CH00692581

ELLY REDDING is an award-wi[n] originally written screenplays, her the Festival of Romance's New Ta

the Independent Author Book Award words for the wounded, as well as being voted Chill with a Book Readers' Book of the Month Award and receiving a B.R.A.G. Medallion.

Born in London, she now divides her time with her husband between Bedfordshire and Devon, where she loves art, dancing and watching the waves.

Elly is a member of the Society of Authors and Alliance of Independent Authors, and would love to hear from you. She can be found @ellyredding on Twitter, Elly Redding Author on Facebook and Elly Redding on Instagram.

To find out more about Elly visit her website ellyredding.com

in too deep

Elly Redding

SilverWood

Published in 2020 by SilverWood Books

SilverWood Books Ltd
14 Small Street, Bristol, BS1 1DE, United Kingdom
www.silverwoodbooks.co.uk

ISBN 978-1-78132-948-1 (paperback)
ISBN 978-1-78132-949-8 (ebook)

British Library Cataloguing in Publication Data
A CIP catalogue record for this book is available from
the British Library

Page design and typesetting by SilverWood Books
Printed on responsibly sourced paper

To Mark, with all my love

Love is knowing that even when you are alone, you will never be lonely again. And great happiness of life is the conviction that we are loved. Loved for ourselves. And even loved in spite of ourselves.

Les Misérables – Victor Hugo

Chapter 1

Isy hated hospitals. She always had. And now here she was charging down some corridor in the middle of the night trying to find the coronary care unit. 'It's all right,' Jack had said on the phone. 'Your father's had a heart attack but you're not to worry…'

Not to worry? She glanced up at the myriad of signs. How could she not worry? Her dear, gentle father, whom she'd hardly seen in the past six years, was ill. Stuck, somewhere, in this labyrinth of a building, while she was going round and round in circles trying to find him.

'Follow the signs,' Jack had said, 'and you can't miss it.'

'Well, I've got news for you,' she muttered, as she rushed back up the flight of stairs she'd just descended, 'it's not as easy as you think.' Which didn't surprise her, as nothing Jack had ever said or done was easy. And as she tore round yet another corner, she knew that better than most. Living with the guy had been an interesting experience and not one she was in a hurry to repeat. After all, who'd want chaos and confusion…

'Isy?'

…when they could have Tom?

'Isy? You're going in completely the wrong direction.'

Spinning round on her heels, she came to a complete halt while the one man she'd just catapulted into obscurity appeared before her, looking annoyingly calm.

'Jack?' she gasped, wondering why her conjuring powers never seemed to get it right. 'You scared me half to death. What do you think you're doing here?'

'Rescuing you, by the looks of it. Coronary Care is this way.'

'I know that,' she said, wishing for once in her life she actually did. 'I was looking for the Ladies'.'

'Which also happens to be this way. Don't ask me how I know. Just accept that I do.'

At that point she wasn't sure she was capable of accepting anything. She was staring straight up at her past, into the devilishly attractive eyes of the man she'd once adored. 'I wasn't expecting you to still be here,' she countered, trying hard not to panic.

'I did say I'd wait.'

'I know, but…'

'You'd rather I hadn't?'

'Something like that. Only, please,' she added quickly, 'don't take it personally.' Actually, on reflection, he could take it as personally as he wanted. That was his penance for turning up here tonight, looking so…so…Jack-like. Gone were the warts and paunch of her daytime meanderings, the double chin, and pencilled in debauchery. And in their place was the disarmingly dishevelled, yet fully toned figure of the man she'd left behind.

'How's Dad?' she asked, desperate to divert her thoughts, and get them back to the only thing that really mattered.

'He's asleep, but he's going to be ok. So, if you want to go home and see him in the morning?'

Only she didn't. She'd come too far. 'I have to see him now. Please? Just a glance?' She blinked back the tears and hoped he'd understand. That for once in their lives, he'd do as she asked, because she didn't have the energy to argue.

She was still reeling from the news, let alone hearing Jack's voice on the phone. From the guilt of knowing she should have come home sooner. That she should have found some way to face her past. But she hadn't. She'd taken the coward's way out and cut herself off. For a few heart-stopping moments earlier today, the incision had almost been permanent.

Jack stood back and let Isy slip into the coronary care unit without him. He watched as she approached a nurse and was directed towards a bed by the window, his attention taken up by every move, every contour of that all too sensual body. And when it was more than he could bear, he forced himself to walk away towards a row of plastic chairs.

So, this is how it's to be, is it? he cursed, sinking down onto one of them. Not a word to him since she'd left Devon for the bright lights of London. And yet, within five seconds of seeing her tonight, it was as though she'd never been away; his mind taking him back to the very first night they'd met, when her father had finally brought him home to Hambledon Hall.

'This is Jack,' Frank was saying, looking up at his daughter from the bottom of the staircase. 'He's going to stay with us for a while... Isy, are you listening?'

But she wasn't, Jack could tell. She was six years old and boys of eleven held little interest for her. She seemed far more interested in how to get herself and her fancy petticoats over the banister. She didn't turn to see a young lad from London looking up at her, with his holdall over his shoulder. Or notice his mouth fall open as she threw herself onto the banister and came sliding down towards them.

'Isabella! Really!' her father protested. But she didn't seem to care. She was whooping like a banshee, her hair a mass of curls, the colour of chestnut.

Seconds later she catapulted off the end and straight into Jack's arms.

Her father shook his head in despair. 'You really should have let her fall,' he said. 'How is she ever going to learn if we keep catching her?'

But Jack wasn't listening. He was looking into a pair of cat's eyes, as green as the emerald on her dress.

'I'm Isy,' she said, as she wriggled out of his arms and onto the ground. 'And you rescued me from pirates.'

Jack looked up the stairs.

'They've gone now, silly,' she admonished. 'But they'll be back. So, we have to be quick,' she said, grabbing his hand and dragging him towards the study. 'They want these.' She produced a pair of pearl earrings. 'They're my mummy's and I have to hide them.'

'Won't your father want them back?' Jack asked, throwing Frank a puzzled glance over his shoulder.

She stopped still in her tracks. 'He's a man, silly, he can't wear them, now can he?'

'No, I meant...'

'And Mummy's dead, so she can't wear them.' Then, as though something had just occurred to her, 'Do you want them – do *you* want to wear my mummy's earrings?'

And despite everything he'd been through, he found himself smiling. It was impossible to do anything else.

'I'm ready.'

Jack opened his eyes. Isy was staring down at him. Only there was no joy in her gaze tonight. No excitement or eager curiosity. Just a flicker of pain as they acknowledged each other with the slightest of smiles.

'Must have nodded off,' he said, pulling himself back up and onto his feet. Not surprising really. He'd been up since before daybreak and it was now two in the morning. 'Do you want a drink or something?'

She shook her head and drew her cardigan around her. It was too large for her and hung haphazardly over her jeans, but it gave her comfort. He could see that. It was the nearest thing to a hug, and, on tonight of all nights, he was glad she at least had that. 'Shall we go then?'

'Where to?' she asked, looking up at him with those large cat's eyes. 'Where are you living now?'

'I'm still with your father, up at the Hall,' he said, leading her back along the deserted corridors and towards the exit.

'What about the cottages?'

'He's rented them out, both of them.'

She glanced back up at him and he had a strong feeling he knew what was coming next. 'That doesn't leave me with too many options then, does it?' she said, with that hint of mischief he'd missed so much. 'You'll have to move out.'

And he was right. 'So,' he said, not entirely sure he followed her logic, 'you want me to move out, do you? Out of a house with eight bedrooms?'

She nodded. 'I think it would be for the best, don't you?'

'And if I don't want to? If my options are – how shall I put it – slightly limited too?'

'Oh, Jack, please. You don't expect me to believe that, do you? Not if what I've heard is true?'

'And what would that be?'

'Wouldn't you like to know? Of course, if I'm wrong…'

'Which you invariably are…'

'Then there must be a string of other women in Branham who'd be only too happy to welcome you into their beds. Of course, I'm not so sure about the men. However, if that's what floats your boat these days, please don't let me stop you.'

'Do you know something?' he said, trying to resist the urge to show her exactly what floated his boat. 'You're as bloody annoying now as you were before you left six years ago.'

'I know.' And the smile that had kept him sane, when nothing else would, broke through. In spite of everything, he couldn't help but reciprocate.

'You've been listening to idle gossip,' he said, as they stopped by the exit. 'But there is something you should know, before you make me homeless. Something which just might make you change your mind.'

'And what would that be?'

'I'll tell you in the morning.'

'But it's morning now?'

'I'll tell you in the morning,' he repeated wishing she'd move away, just a little. That she'd stop looking up at him like that, with such an indignant tilt to those lips, that just made them all the more enticing.

'And what if I don't want to – wait until the morning that is?'

'Then you'll have to sleep with me, Isy, because that's the only way you're going to get any information out of me tonight.' And since he didn't know where the hell that had come from, he prayed she'd drop the inquisition, and help him find her car instead.

Isy could have hit him, if she was the hitting type – which she wasn't – but she was seriously considering making this an exception. What had he thought he was doing, teasing her about their past on today of all days? Why couldn't he have just answered the question? Or told her, very politely, to shut up? Because the last thing she needed right now was to focus on his bedroom, let alone his bed.

This was why she'd not come home. Why she'd done what he'd told her and set herself free. No communication. No memories. No Jack. And not even her father could persuade her otherwise.

'You should at least talk to him, my dear,' he'd suggest when they chatted on the phone. 'Let him know you're happy, that there are no hard feelings?' But she couldn't. Not because she wasn't happy, because she was. She'd worked really hard to turn her life around and she'd succeeded. She was a qualified solicitor with an equally successful boyfriend, but she could play at mind games too. In fact, she'd become really rather good at them since she'd left, which was just as well as she was going to need all the help she could get, if she was going to survive being under the same roof as Jack.

Hambledon Hall might have eight bedrooms. It might have three floors and a cellar for storing the wine. Six acres of land and a stunning sea view. Not to mention a roof which leaked, and a Georgian façade to die for. But it was still too small to house the pair of them, together. And there was nothing, absolutely nothing, that Jack, her father, or anyone else could say or do that would make her change her mind.

Chapter 2

Six years was a long time to be away and Isy had forgotten how dark Devon could be. How narrow the lanes were, as she edged the Mini deeper and deeper into the countryside. Cottages, shrouded by the night, were dotted along the route, with little sign of life; just the light on Jack's motorbike flashing at her as it snaked its way around the bends. Until, finally, it disappeared altogether, leaving her very much alone.

She was going home, but it wasn't the homecoming she'd have wished for. There'd be no welcome party. No father standing on the steps, by the portico, with his arms outstretched. And she couldn't believe how stupid she'd been. How naïve to have thought that nothing would change. Only she'd been so busy struggling to survive herself, it had never occurred to her that others might not. That her father wasn't indestructible, the realisation causing such a spasm of pain to well up inside her, that it was all she could do not to give in and let it all out.

'Grief is good,' she told herself, recalling one of the numerous self-help books she'd flicked through during the past few years. 'Emotions are positive.' Only she wasn't entirely sure how helpful that was here, as the last thing she was going to do was turn up at the Hall sobbing hysterically.

She didn't need Jack's sympathy, or anything else for that matter. She'd managed very well without him these past six years, and she certainly didn't need him now. The man who'd offered her the world, only for her to discover it had never really included her. How could she ever have thought she'd needed a guy like that? When, deep down, she was scared he'd never really left. That he was still there somewhere, tucked away in a special corner of her heart.

'Isy, are you listening to me?'

No, no, I'm not, she wanted to shout back. *I'm not in the mood for memories.* Only it was hard to shut them out, the closer to home she came. Jack's voice was as clear to her tonight, as it was back then, when the only thing she'd had to worry about was trying to find a signal for her phone.

'You're going to break your neck. Isy, for Christ's sake, it's dark out there. There are rabbit holes everywhere. At least wait for me to find my boots.'

'I'll be fine,' she'd yelled back at him, pointing her mobile towards the stars. And she was, until the time no one told her about some posts and a freshly dug trench.

'Now perhaps you'll listen to us,' her father remonstrated, while she nursed a sprained ankle and a bump on her head the size of a lemon. 'It could have been so much worse.'

She wasn't sure she agreed. In her view, it could have been so much better. That only an idiot would leave a trench uncovered, but she didn't argue. Instead, she hitched a lift with Jack into Exeter, to buy some much-needed provisions.

'This should do the trick,' she said, producing the largest torch she could find and a couple of very sturdy crutches.

'And if not,' Jack replied, 'there's always plan B.' Which, she soon discovered, was building a small platform at just the right spot to capture the signal. 'To stop you from disappearing for good,' he confirmed, as he mapped out a path to it with some low-level lights.

Isy smiled. 'Are you sure you're not compensating for something?' she teased, as the design took on an interesting shape.

She was fourteen and he was nineteen. He was the best looking guy for miles around, with his dark olive skin and inquisitive brows, and all her friends fancied him like crazy. 'Can't you put in a good word for us,' they'd beg, and she tried. She really did, but Jack never appeared to be interested. Not in her friends. Not even in Jess, who was petite, blonde, and beautiful, with a personality to match.

'You don't think he's…um…gay?' Jess had asked once when her charms had failed to impress.

Isy almost burst out laughing. *No,* she wanted to say, having seen him with a girl she didn't recognise only yesterday. 'I wouldn't worry though,' she assured Jess. 'You wouldn't want him, anyway. He's really bad on the phone. No chat at all.'

Since Jess lived on her mobile, signal or not, Isy hoped that would soften the blow. And it did, for a while. Only now, thirteen years later, they were an item, according to a recent posting on Facebook. Isy doubted whether Jack knew social media existed.

Or that Jess had broadcast their relationship to the world. However, the fact was things had changed. That they'd changed and Isy had never felt more like a stranger in her life.

And in a few minutes time, everything was going to get a whole lot worse. There'd be no turning back. No retreat, as she pulled in through those pillars of stone. She'd have to talk to Jack. Breathe the same air as him and go to sleep knowing his bedroom was only a corridor away.

If that wasn't enough to make her turn around, and head straight back to the hospital, she wasn't sure what would.

Jack was pacing up and down. He didn't know what else to do. His feet were pounding across the well-trod flagstones of the hallway as though, somehow, that energy would transform into action. That by sheer willpower alone, she'd appear before him.

It was the moment he'd been waiting for ever since she'd left. His chance to make amends. And he didn't know when he'd been more nervous.

'Is this what you really want?' she'd asked, as he'd stood aside to let her go. 'Because, if it is, you'll never see or hear from me again.' His feet wavering on one side of the front door, while hers stood firm on the other. 'I thought you loved me,' she'd said. 'That there was nothing we couldn't share, but I was wrong. I thought you trusted me with the truth.'

Her words still hit him where it hurt. How could he trust her with the truth, the whole truth, when he didn't trust himself? He couldn't. That's why he'd let her go. Why he'd not run after her and begged her to stay. But there'd not been a moment since when he didn't regret it, his heart reverberating against his ribcage, like some lovesick teenager, rather than the disillusioned man he'd become.

Six years was a hell of a long time to dream. To curse himself for what he'd done. But now she was back, he finally had a chance to put things right. And he owed it to himself, to both of them, not to screw it up again.

'What happened to the drive back there?' Isy exclaimed, rescuing her overnight bag from the boot of the car. 'It forked off to the left and I almost followed it.' She glanced up at the man beside her, at that dark hair and stubble. 'Don't suppose it would have anything to do with what you wanted to talk to me about in the morning, would it?'

He held out his hand to take her bag from her. 'You don't give up, do you?'

'No, never,' she replied, clinging on resolutely to her belongings. Or, at least, she would have done so, if she hadn't spotted something else; a sinister shape in the dark, looking vaguely like a skip. And she was just about to crunch her way across the gravel to investigate, when she realised Jack had taken her bag, and was heading off in the opposite direction, along with the torch.

'Are there any other little surprises I should know about?' she asked, as he waited for her to climb the steps of the portico before him. 'No unexpected sleeping partners, perhaps? Girlfriends smuggled in, then forgotten about?'

'Not tonight,' he acknowledged with a ghost of a smile. 'Unless there's something you know, that I don't?'

Not on your life, she wanted to say, but she didn't. She just gave him the most charming smile she could conjure up at four in the morning. 'I'm so glad it's just you. I would hate to have to evict more than one of you in the morning. Might get myself a reputation!'

There, she congratulated herself. She'd done it. She'd crossed over the threshold with her sanity still intact. Just. The glow from the table lamps welcomed her. Perfectly balanced shades, on an explosion of blue-and-white porcelain, stood proud on dust-covered tables, while the walls reached up to the plaster friezes and the roof beyond.

And there, on those walls, hung a display of paintings of every shape and size. Splashes of colour which were as brilliant as light itself and just as powerful. Even in the gloom, Isy could still feel their presence. These were oils painted by her mother, a woman she'd never really known. And for a few minutes, it was all she could do to stand and stare. To soak up what little comfort she could, before it was snatched away again from her forever.

'The water should still be hot.' Jack's voice was saying somewhere in the background. 'I left the immersion on. I can run a bath for you, if you like?'

Normally just the thought of that would have sent her scurrying for the latest hyperbole on hell and the art of freezing, but not tonight. The kindness in his words made her want to hug him instead.

'Thank you,' she said, turning to him in the half-light, 'but I'll be fine.'

She stretched out her hand to take her bag from him. He

22

hesitated, and she could sense the indecision running through his thoughts. As though he, too, was trying to write some rules, which they both knew would be totally disregarded at the first possible opportunity.

'Wouldn't want you to lose your beauty sleep on my account,' she teased as lightly as she could. 'And besides, there's breakfast to cook tomorrow. I still burn everything.'

His response was fleeting: a raised eyebrow, the slightest of grins. But it was so inclusive, she couldn't shut it out, no matter how hard she tried. 'So, you do have a use for me,' he said as he handed her the bag, and she felt his fingers brush briefly, oh so briefly, against hers. 'Let's hope I don't disappoint then, shall we?'

As if you could, a voice said from nowhere. Only it wasn't hers. It was a ghost from the past and she knew she should turn around and flee to anywhere but here, but she didn't know whether her legs would carry her. She was having enough difficulty reaching the stairs, let alone the world outside.

Think of Tom, she told herself sternly. Think of the man sleeping in your bed in London tonight, each blond hair neatly in its place. Think of him and not the one who's watching you, almost willing you to turn around, with those eyes of liquid gold.

It was only when she'd reached the landing, and could almost feel the distance between them, that she dared risk another glance. Jack was still standing exactly where she'd left him. The unanswered question still lingering on his lips, which she knew had absolutely nothing to do with baths or breakfast, and that made her grab for her mobile.

Three texts, four missed calls, and one slightly irate email. All received before she'd left the hospital, but she didn't care. It was the equivalent of a goodnight kiss, a reminder she still had London. And first thing tomorrow morning, or rather today, she would tell Tom just how grateful she was for that. How she'd never fall asleep during one of his lectures on procurement again.

Now, though, she had some frantic rebuilding to do, to repair her shattered nerves with a good dose of common sense. And then, if that failed, to find a key. Although whether she was locking Jack out of her old bedroom, or herself in, she wasn't entirely sure. All she knew, as she sought sanctuary against the soft pillows and sweet smell of her duvet, was that she was home. And to her dismay, it felt surprisingly good.

Chapter 3

Several hours later and Isy wasn't so sure. Sleep had been sporadic, her dreams punctuated with a lifetime of memories. Many of which she could have done without. And Tom's interrogation at nine the following morning certainly wasn't helping.

'Where the hell are you, Bella?' he enquired, his clipped Etonian vowels resonating at her down the landline. 'Outer bloody Mongolia?'

'Not exactly,' she began, but she might as well have been. Cradling the handset under a duvet wigwam probably wasn't one of her more inspired ideas either, but she'd absolutely no intention of leaving her bedroom again. She'd done it once, to call the hospital, and she'd got away with it. No Jack. Next time she might not be so lucky.

'Bella, are you there?'

'Of course I am.'

'Not one response, Bella. Not one. I even tried the number you're on now, but nothing. Absolutely nothing.'

'That's probably because I was still with Dad.'

'And later?'

'Later? Well, later…it's…it's complicated,' she finished lamely, grateful for the lack of FaceTime.

Jack, of course, would have asked her, 'How complicated?' He'd have reeled her in like the prize idiot she was and watched with amusement as she struggled to extricate herself. But Tom wasn't like that, especially when he had some news of his own to impart. 'I had something to tell you, Bella. Something so important it couldn't wait…'

She lowered the handset and wondered. Was this it? Was this the moment she'd been waiting for – for the past two years? When he'd finally tell her he loved her? That he wanted to marry her? To give her babies? Lots and lots of lovely little Toms?

'I've been made a partner,' he said as she raised the piece of plastic back to her ear. 'Wicked, eh? What do you say?'

'Say?' she repeated numbly, trying to bump start her brain into something resembling conversation. Say? What could she say, as she watched all her dreams fly out of the window again? 'I say, it's…it's great. Marvellous. We should celebrate,' she added, trying to sound as enthusiastic as he was.

'Too right we will. When are you coming back, Bella? I miss you.'

'I miss you too, but…'

'But what?'

But someone else had just entered the bedroom. Someone who obviously couldn't read, since they'd just ignored the very large *Keep Out* sign she'd been forced to stick to the door, in the absence of any key. And who now was probably toying with a million and one ways to annoy her, rather than doing the decent thing and leaving her alone.

'But what?' Tom reiterated.

'But I've got to go...' she said as quickly as she could. She could feel a tap on her head, as though she were an egg about to be cracked. 'Go away,' she muttered as an indignant 'Bella' echoed at her in response. 'Not you,' she hissed down the line, 'you I love. Whereas you,' she said, addressing the man peeling the duvet away from her head and face, 'I could honestly do without. I am now cold, or didn't it occur to you that there might be a reason for my dress code?'

Jack didn't flinch. 'Why are you sitting like an Indian squaw, perched on the middle of your bed, holding court?' he asked, the corners of his mouth twitching as he surveyed the scene in front of him.

'I'm not an Indian squaw.'

'But you're sitting in the middle of your bed, holding the phone. Did you get through to the hospital?'

She nodded. 'He's had a good night and is looking forward to seeing us...me,' she quickly corrected herself, 'this afternoon.'

'And lover boy?' he added with more than a hint of amusement. 'Assuming that's who you were speaking to. Did he say he loved you back?'

She quickly checked to make sure she was properly disconnected. 'And since when did you become my confidante?' she asked, when she was sure it was just the two of them.

'He didn't, did he?'

'Actually, he did,' she said, rising to meet his challenge. 'He says it all the time.' *Just like you used to,* she wanted to add, catching the dangerous glint smouldering in those eyes. *When you'd scoop me up off this bed and show me exactly how much you cared.*

Only it wasn't true, none of it. They were words, just words, nothing more. As empty as the nights which had followed, when she'd lain alone in a strange city, wishing he was there beside her. That he'd be the man she'd always thought he was.

'Why are you really here?' she asked, trying to get back to the present.

'We've got a date.'

'We have?'

'Breakfast and an explanation,' he added, turning up her radiator. 'Or have you forgotten?'

Jack surveyed the scene before him. The bacon was crisp but not burnt, just the way she liked it. The bread was fresh from the village bakery. And the kitchen was in dire need of a revamp. Shaker in style, where there was one. The rest of it was an eclectic mix of eras, dating back, he guessed, to pre-war. Something else to add to the list, he decided, along with wondering what the hell to do about Isy.

Friends? Was that *ever* conceivably possible? A pie crust promise made to himself, at the depths of despair, when he'd have done anything to see her, just for a day. Only, when he'd found her sitting there on that bed, it wasn't friendship he'd wanted, it was love. He'd wanted to lavish those lips with a lifetime of longing and that body with a damn sight more.

God, how he'd missed her, that air of defiance. That sense of loyalty, that sprang up out of nowhere, when you were least expecting it, sending him straight back to his past. To a cold, cloudy night in June, when she was just sixteen, and all he'd wanted was to be left alone.

'I thought I'd find you here,' Isy was saying, but Jack wasn't listening. He had other things to think about back then. So, he continued sitting where he was, in his jeans and a T-shirt, on a cold, clammy rock, staring out to sea. Wondering how it would feel to walk towards the waves, to keep on walking, and never look back.

'Jack?' Her voice drifted in and out of his thoughts. 'Do you want me to go away? Only Dad said you'd had some bad news, but he wouldn't say what. And I thought you might like to talk about it?' She paused as if to gauge his reaction. 'Do you want to talk to me about it?'

'No,' he managed to get out. 'Now, will you piss off and leave me alone?'

'Nope,' she said, sitting down on the rock beside him. 'Everyone needs a friend, and you're particularly lucky, because you've got me, whether you want me or not.'

She slipped her arm through his, and for a few minutes he fought against every instinct he had for self-preservation. Against the need to lash out and hurt her, as he was hurting, deep down inside. But he couldn't; he couldn't do anything to hurt her. She was the sister he'd never had, as precious to him as the air she breathed.

And so he allowed her to stay where she was and cuddle up against him, the silence between them stretching out as far as the sea. Until, finally, she gave his arm an affectionate squeeze. 'We should do this more often,' she said, as though it was the most natural thing in the world.

He risked a glance at her. 'Even if it's starting to rain?'

'Even if it's starting to rain, because one day it won't be, and you wouldn't want to miss out on that, now would you?' She beamed up at him with so much hope in those eyes that he could have kissed her. He could have taken all that energy and turned it into something far more than brotherly love. And the thought scared him witless as he realised that what he'd begun to fear might well be true.

'You've got your end-of-year prom in two weeks,' he said, trying to crush his libido with a quick check on reality. 'We should be getting back. Don't want you to catch a cold.'

But she wouldn't let him go. 'A few drops of rain won't hurt us, will they? And besides, I've not told you my news. Jess is going to invite you to her sixteenth birthday party!'

He drew in a muted sigh of exasperation. 'I'm not going out with her, Isy, before you ask me again.'

'Who – me?' she queried, with a mischievous glance. 'As if I would, but I've got something else to tell you too.' Jumping up, she gave him the benefit of a mock drum roll. 'I've been asked to play Juliet in the school play next term. Isn't that cool?'

He wasn't sure if it was cool, hot, or downright boiling. All he could think about was who the hell would be playing Romeo?

'Pete Pinkerton!' she said, as though she could read his mind.

'The guy who snorts when he laughs?'

'I know. Gross, isn't it? How can I possibly declare my undying love to him? It's like playing opposite a pig!'

He couldn't help but laugh. More with relief, than he'd have liked.

'So,' she said, as she pulled him up and onto his feet. 'This is the moment you've been waiting for all your life. How's your Shakespeare?'

'My what?'

'Your Shakespeare, idiot. The author of the play. I need to practise my lines and I don't think Dad's a very good substitute for Romeo, do you?'

'Isy…'

'I know, I know, anyone's better than poor old Pinkerton, but if I've got to declare my undying love for anyone, who better than you? What do you think?' she asked, clasping his hand to her heart, before he could resist. 'Will you die for me, Jack? Will you be my one and only true love – my very own Romeo?'

A few months later and Jack was wishing he'd said no. Or, at least, asked for a recast. The trouble was Isy was just too damn good at her role. So that every time she looked up at him, with that twinkle in her eyes, he wanted to forget everything he'd told himself. How it was only a passing fancy. That he was mad to even contemplate it, because he wanted to play Romeo for real. He wanted to show that Pinkerton guy how to woo her, if only to find a reason for this madness, because madness was what it was.

He was finally acknowledging the truth, God help him. That Romeo might end up taking his own life, but he wasn't ready to let go of his. He had a reason for living and he was looking straight at it. A reason to hope, in his bruised and battered heart, that one day she might, just might, feel the same way about him.

'Jack?'

He glanced across at the kitchen doorway. Not today she didn't. The contrast with the past couldn't have been more striking. She was standing, staring straight at him, but there was no desire in her eyes, just curiosity. No lust or love on those lips, as immaculate as ever, with just a splash of colour. There wasn't even friendship.

And he knew, as he handed her a bacon butty, that what he said in the next few minutes was as important as how he'd behaved all those years ago. Only this time, the goal was to avoid eviction.

Chapter 4

'Why didn't Dad tell me?' Isy moaned, as she tried to take in what Jack was telling her. 'When we met at my aunt's last year? When we spoke on the phone? Why didn't he let me know what was going on? Because I could have helped. I know I could, if only I'd known.'

'Don't blame yourself. What's happened isn't your fault.'

'Isn't it?'

'No, it's not,' Jack stated emphatically. 'You can't blame yourself for genetics. Your dad's had a heart attack, a blockage in his artery. You didn't cause that.'

She looked across the table to where he was sitting. This was the man she'd tried so hard to hate, and he was being kind to her. It was the worst kind of punishment.

'Why didn't you tell me about what was happening?' she asked, trying again to redress the balance. 'About the money – or rather the lack of it. The wedding venue idea? The house restoration? You could have told me…'

'And how was I supposed to do that, exactly? You'd blocked me from any form of communication, in case you've forgotten, let alone anything else.'

'That's not true. I spoke to you yesterday.'

'Only because I told your receptionist it was about your father.'

'See!' She seized on his last words, as though she were back at work, and she'd just seen a fundamental flaw in the other side's argument. 'You could have phoned. You could have told me it was about my father, but you didn't.'

'And what would you have done if I had?' he retaliated. 'Would you have given up your life in London to return here? To help us out with the venture? To be near me?'

'Of course I would,' she declared, incensed he could think anything else. 'I'd do anything for my father. You know I would.' But even as she voiced the words, and braved the honesty in his, she knew he was right. She loved her father to bits, but would she have come home? Would she have forced herself to face Jack, when she knew there was a way to avoid it?

'I *am* a bad person,' she said, wishing with all her heart it wasn't true, 'and there's nothing you can say to make me change my mind. Because if I wasn't, Dad would have told me, wouldn't he? And he didn't, because he knew what I'd say, that I'd tell him to sell.'

He didn't speak. Instead, he reached out his hand to her from across the table. And she knew she should take it. That she should seize this chance to reconcile their differences, but she couldn't. If she touched his flesh and felt the strength of his grip in hers, she'd be saying it was all right. That *they* were all right. But they weren't. How could they possibly be, when it was thanks to him that she was in this situation in the first place?

'What I don't get,' she said, trying desperately to hang on to those bits she did understand, 'is why Dad's so hard up for money?

I know building work dried up after the recession, that there wasn't enough for both of you, but my great-grandparents bought this place outright. So why can't he borrow against that?'

'I think this is a discussion you should be having with your father, don't you? But not this afternoon,' he added quickly, in case she thought she should.

She couldn't help but look surprised. 'Do you really think I'm that thoughtless?' she asked, as he stood up to replenish their drinks.

'Yes, yes, I do, when you're on a mission. Or at least you used to be.'

And she was about to dispute that and tell him it was a gross misinterpretation of her childhood let alone the facts, when she had to concede he did have a point.

'OK,' she said, as he handed her back a fresh mug of coffee. 'Leaving the past to one side, I assume you have a plan?'

'Of course.'

'And?'

'I stay here, and you do what I tell you to do.'

'Not such a great fan of that.'

'Which bit?' he asked.

'Both.'

'In which case, do you have a better one?'

'Naturally,' she said, trying to think on her feet. 'How about you move out while I come up with one?'

He laughed. 'Good try, Isy,' he acknowledged, 'but it won't work, and I'll tell you why, because there isn't time. We have three months, just three months, to finish restoring this place. To get it ready for a trial run with Mrs White's golden wedding anniversary party just before Christmas. Then, if all goes well for your father's old housekeeper, we'll apply for a licence to do weddings in the New Year.'

'Three months?' She was still stuck on the timeframe. The rest of his explanation could have been in Mandarin for all she knew, and no matter how hard she tried to move herself forwards, to see the bigger picture, she kept coming back to that. 'And you can't change it – the deadline? You can't push it into the New Year?'

'Not if we want to keep the Hall. We have to stick to the plan.'

Which gave her the answer she'd feared, as her diary and a multitude of complications flashed up before her. And she didn't know what to say, or do, without sounding like the worst daughter in the world, which she wasn't. Only she had responsibilities, too, back in London. She had a duty of care to her firm, her clients, and to Tom. And the more she thought about how to juggle the logistics, the more it tore her apart. The agony of, once again, trying to get it right.

'You need to make your mind up.' Only this time Jack wasn't standing where she'd left him, in her father's kitchen. They were both in her cramped flat in Sheffield, during her last term at uni. Her very own Ghostbuster, or so she used to think, who never let her down. Not even when he was on a promise back in Devon.

'About what?' she asked, staring up at him from where she was sitting on her bed. 'What do I have to make my mind up about?'

'About whether you want me to go and beat him up for you?'

'And you'd do that for me, would you?' she asked in cautious admiration. 'Beat up the captain of this year's rugby team?'

'Of course. I'm a bit rusty. Not beaten anyone up for a while, but I'm sure it'll come back to me,' he said, with that attractive twist of those lips. And she knew he was joking, but it did have a certain heroic twang to it, which she was finding slightly harder to dismiss.

'He said I was difficult,' she sniffed, staring down at a pile of disintegrating tissues. 'That I didn't give him his space. Well, I did, Jack, I really did. I gave him all the space I could find but then he went and shared it with somebody else. A guy – I've been dumped for a guy!'

To his credit, he didn't laugh, and she could have hugged him for that alone.

'Look,' he said, coming to sit down on the bed next to her, 'you're as fresh, beautiful, and feminine as they come. And if he couldn't appreciate that, because you just happen to be the wrong sex, then that's his loss, not yours.'

'You forgot intelligent,' she prompted. 'Am I really all those things?'

The corners of his mouth twitched. 'You know you are.'

'Then why can't I find someone like you, who actually appreciates me?'

'Possibly because I'm unique?' Only he wasn't looking at her, as he usually did, with that sense of self-mockery. He was studying her duvet as though it held the answer to the Holy Grail.

'So,' she said, squeezing his hand tightly, to get his attention. 'I'm sorry about your hot date.' He raised his eyes. 'Jess told me,' she explained. 'She also told me you're taking her out next week?'

'To see Muse at Torquay. And that's *not* a date, Isy, before you ask.'

'Are you sure about that?' she asked, catching his gaze.

'Would you mind if it was?'

'No, why should I?'

'No reason.'

Only, suddenly, she did. Suddenly she minded desperately, and she wasn't sure where the thought had come from, or why it wouldn't go away. But it wouldn't. And for the first time she found herself wondering if she'd got it wrong? If what she'd always wanted for Jess, was actually what she'd wanted for herself? A shift so seismic in its implications, that she retrieved her fingers as quickly as she could, before they could get her into any more trouble.

'I need to blow my nose,' she said, trying to justify her actions by grabbing the box of tissues on the bed next to him. Her eyes drifted back up at him, at the guarded expression on his face.

Once she would have asked, 'Why are you looking at me like that?' But not now. Now she wanted to seduce him rather than question him. To pull him down on the bed beside her and do all the things that prat, Miles Banyard, had done to her. But she knew Jack would never agree to that. That he'd sooner have her committed for insanity than make love to her, and he was probably right.

'I should be getting back,' he said, as though he knew exactly what she was thinking. 'It's getting late.'

Only she wasn't ready for him to leave. 'Let's run away together. Let's get on your bike and go somewhere now. You and me... Together... What do you say?'

'What do I say?' He sounded as though he was having extreme

difficulty in saying anything. 'And where exactly do you want to go?' he managed to get out, finally.

'Anywhere. Anywhere you like. Have you got your passport?'

'No. Have you got yours?'

'Yes, of course. I used to be in the Brownies, remember?'

He raised a bemused eyebrow. 'Before they kicked you out for setting fire to a tent.'

'I don't think they were ready for me.'

'I don't think anyone ever is.' And with that, he reached out and retrieved her hand in his. A gesture that sent her heart somersaulting into a gymnastic display all of its very own. 'Are you serious?' he asked, narrowing his gaze. His whole presence so close, that it was all she could do to think, let alone remember who he was... Her surrogate brother... Her childhood friend... The man she mustn't fuck.

'Totally serious,' she declared, trying not to blush.

'Then, if you still want to go away with me next year,' he said, with more enthusiasm than she was expecting, 'I'll take you wherever you want to go. I promise. If you don't get your training contract, I'll show you the world.'

'Only you never did.'

'What?'

She glanced up at him. *You never did show me the world. You broke my heart instead.*

'Are you all right?'

No, no, I'm not. How can I be when you're standing there, in my father's kitchen, looking at me as though you actually care?

'I was just remembering something,' she said quickly, 'but it's not important. It's really not.'

'Good,' he said, gently removing the mug from her hands, 'because I've got something to show you which is.' Leaning towards her, he pulled her to her feet. She didn't argue, although she knew she could. She was too busy trying not to react to his touch, to the warmth of his fingers against hers.

So, she focussed on everything except him as he led her away from the inviting smell of bacon and coffee, and out into the hall. Through the main drawing room, where the walls were ready for rewiring, with channels carved out of the brick, and on until they reached her father's study. A room where vistas opened up on adjoining sides, and metres of crushed velvet cascaded down from the pelmets onto the floor beneath.

'This is where he works,' he said, looking at the two desks, piled high with paperwork, 'until late at night, trying to sort out this mess, to safeguard your mother's inheritance, as well as everything else.'

'Please, please, don't do this to me,' she protested, 'because I feel guilty enough without you making me feel worse.'

'I know you do,' he said, softening his tone, 'but guilt isn't going to change the situation, is it? We need to find a way to help him. And if I thought I could do it alone, I would. There's no way, no bloody way, I want to wake up every morning, knowing how you must feel about me. That you hate my guts. But this is your home, Isy, your heritage, and I can't save it by myself. Not anymore. I need help.'

She glanced up at him. 'Are you asking me what I think you're asking me?'

His jawline tightened. 'Yes.'

'Even after everything that's happened?'

He gave her the briefest of nods. 'Because it's not about us, anymore, is it? It's about your father. And he's got to come first.'

Of course he did; she was annoyed that he could even think otherwise. Her only problem, now, though, was trying to work out how to make that happen. How to keep Tom and her father happy, as well as her firm.

And Jack? What *was* she going to do about Jack? The man who was looking at her as though he didn't know whether to run for the hills or crack open the champagne? And she wished it wasn't so, that she could tell him it would be all right. That it had to be, for her father's sake, but she couldn't, because she didn't have a clue. She was coming home, but she'd never been more uncertain about anything in her entire life.

Jack needed air, plenty of it. He needed to get out and go for a run. Or throw himself into what he should have been doing this morning, finish landscaping the grounds with the aid of a recalcitrant digger he'd called 'Fred'. At that moment, he wasn't too fussy. He just knew he needed to escape. That it would soon be Christmas and Santa was nowhere in bloody sight.

Grabbing his overcoat from the rack in the hall, he shoved his feet into a pair of muddy work boots and opened the front door. In front of him lay the grounds he was struggling to control, gentle undulations of green, dotted about with clumps of trees. And in between, framed to perfection, were snapshots of the sea and the sky beyond, a patch of blue on an otherwise cloudy day.

That Isy could even think of giving all this up, a home that had been in her family for four generations, was beyond him. But then she didn't know what it was to do without. To wake up, day after day, surrounded by debris and confusion.

'Jack?'

A voice interrupted his thoughts, but it wasn't Isy's. Turning round, he could see Jess running towards him across the grass. Long wisps of blonde hair were scrunched up tightly under a slide, while the skirt of her dress, a vintage find from the forties, rose and fell with every step she took.

'We're meant to be meeting with Harry at twelve,' she puffed, once she'd finally caught up with him. 'And you've not been answering your phone.'

He glanced at his watch. 'You'll have to go without me,' he said, as apologetically as he could. 'Make my excuses. You know what we want to do with our new website, what we discussed.'

'Is Isy still here?' she asked in that soft and perfectly poised voice of hers.

He gave her as nonchalant a nod as he could.

'Have you told her about me – that I'm living in one of the cottages?'

'No, not yet, but I will, when the time's right.'

Jess looked as though she didn't quite believe him. And he knew he should confront the concern he could see written all over that pretty face. But he couldn't, as he knew she'd read things into it which wouldn't be fair to any of them.

'Do you want me to go?' she asked.

'To see Harry? Yes. To discuss our profile, our visibility on the net.'

Her forehead creased momentarily. 'You know what I mean.'

He did. He knew exactly what she meant. Only he wasn't having it. Not for a moment. 'You're staying,' he said, as emphatically as he could. 'Isy's the one who's been away, not you. We're not changing anything just because she's back.'

And with a gesture which he hoped would silence her doubts, he went over to where she was standing and kissed her, briefly, on the cheek.

'Good luck,' he said as she smiled in return. 'I'll be at the hospital this afternoon, but I'll come around to see you as usual this evening.'

'And Isy?'

'Isy will be doing what Isy does best.'

'And what is that?'

'I have absolutely no idea.'

Isy was still busy trying to work out strategies. She needed to try to come up with a plan, and preferably before Jack arrived at the hospital with one of his own.

'Dad,' she gasped, once she'd finally found out where they'd moved him. 'Should you be up – in a chair?'

'And should you be here, my dear, in Devon?' The pleasure of her appearance rippled across every wrinkle of that well-loved face. 'I told Jack not to phone you.'

She gave him an affectionate kiss on the cheek, and drew up a chair beside him, suddenly aware she was being looked at by the occupants of the other three beds in the room.

'So, how are you feeling?' she asked, trying to ignore them.

'What did the consultant say? I couldn't find anyone to talk to me.'

Frank put out his hands, etched with years of hard labour, and she grasped them both tightly. It had been such a shock seeing him surrounded by monitors in the coronary care unit, with lines and lights flashing away at her in the dark. Today, though, in a general ward, he was looking more like his old self, with his crop of white hair and workman's physique, a copy of *The Times* resting loosely on his lap, glasses perched precariously at the end of his nose.

'Nothing to worry about,' he said softly, 'I'll be out in a few days.'

'So soon?'

'They just need to check the stent's doing its job, and then I can go.'

She knew she should be pleased at this, to have her father back at the Hall, so she could care for him. But the prospect of him returning to all the chaos far outweighed the benefits. 'I've been giving this some thought,' she said, as gently as she could, 'and I don't think you should come back home. You need to rest.'

'Nonsense,' Frank said more firmly than she was expecting. And she was about to refute this and tell him all about her wonderful plan for his rehabilitation, when Jack appeared out of nowhere.

'Sorry I'm late,' he said, leaning across her to shake Frank's hand. His body, his whole physique, far too close for comfort.

'I'll sit on the bed,' she said, in a desperate attempt to remedy the situation. And to her surprise, Jack didn't resist. He just watched in amusement as she performed a complicated dance to wriggle past every part of his anatomy with the minimum of contact.

'Better?' he asked once she was perched on the bottom of the bed.

'Perfect,' she replied with the sweetest of smiles. 'And you?'

He sat down on the chair. 'It's nice and warm. Can almost feel your presence.'

And if her father hadn't been watching them so intently, she might have told Jack exactly what he could do with that, but right now she needed his support.

'I was just telling Dad he mustn't come home,' she began, praying Jack would follow her lead, 'that it would be far too stressful with everything that's going on.'

'I couldn't agree more. Sorry, Frank, but I'm with Isy on this.'

'You are?' *He was? He was actually agreeing with her?* She gave him a curious stare. Her heart leaping with hope and something else she couldn't quite define.

'It's for the best, Dad,' she said quickly, before the momentum was lost. 'I've phoned Auntie Beth and she said she'd be delighted for you to come and stay. Please say yes?'

Only Frank wasn't looking at her, he was busy looking at Jack. What worried her was that neither of them was looking her way.

'OK, I give up. Will one of you please tell me what's going on here?'

Her father tried to give her a reassuring smile. 'There's nothing for you to worry about, my dear, I was just wondering, if I go to my sister's in Sussex, who is going to look after everything at the Hall?'

'I will,' Jack said, before she could interrupt.

'But what about your other business?'

Other business? Her ears pricked up. 'What other business?'

Jack threw Frank a warning glance, but it was too late. The cat was out of the bag, and she had absolutely no intention of putting it back in.

'What other business?' she repeated, with eager curiosity. 'Jack? Dad? Why will no one talk to me?'

'Have you told your father what *you're* up to?' Jack retaliated, sidestepping the question once again. 'That you're going to stay down here to help us out?'

'No, she hasn't,' Frank answered before she could. 'Is this true, my dear?' he asked, while she threw Jack a glare which would have melted mountains. 'But what about your job in London? And Tom? And what about Jess, Jack? What about the business?'

All excellent questions, she conceded, but she was only really interested in the answer to the last two. It was like *Mastermind* for the dysfunctional, and Jack had the chair, whether he wanted it or not. Nothing else mattered. Not the patients, the faded curtains, or the stench of disinfectant and something else she couldn't quite place. All of this was parked, ushered to the back of her mind, while she waited for him to respond, and offer her something resembling an explanation.

'Jess?' she queried, when he didn't. 'And the business? You were saying?'

'I wasn't,' he responded, with that air of resilience she knew only too well, 'but since you won't let this rest, I'm helping Jess run her company. OK? So now you know.'

Only she didn't. She'd seen Jess's posts on Facebook, about her soaps for sensitive skins, but there'd been no mention of Jack. 'And how are you managing this?'

'With difficulty,' her father supplied when Jack didn't. 'It's really taken off, you see. They're offering others the opportunity to sell their products, too, through their site. We've got cable now, to improve the connection, and factories too. All very exciting, my dear. All very high-tech.'

It sounded like it. It just didn't sound like Jack. He was the boy who was never happier than when he was careering across some rugby field or surfing off the coast. Who'd sailed through his exams with no intention of using them for anything other than to help her father out building homes.

'You'll have to tell me all about it,' she said, 'this new venture of yours.' But before she could prise any further information out of Jack, a nurse arrived to do her father's ECG.

'You're full of surprises,' she said, as they took the opportunity to get themselves a coffee. 'No wonder you need help with everything. Why didn't you tell me about it this morning? That it's not just the restoration that takes up your time, but this business too?'

'This business helps pay for the restoration,' he said simply.

But Isy knew that it was much more than that. That it was probably their main source of income and she loved him for it. However hard she tried to dismiss the thought, and put it back safely where it belonged, she couldn't. She loved the kindness and the inherent goodness she'd forgotten existed.

'Why didn't you tell me about all of this,' she repeated quietly. 'Why didn't you tell me about Jess?'

Jack drained the last of the dregs from his plastic cup, before squeezing it together with his hands and throwing it into the bin.

'We should be getting back.'

But she wasn't finished. 'You want me to stay down here with you? Reorganise my life? Yet still you won't tell me about yours. Do you think that's fair?' she asked, catching his gaze, 'after everything we've been through?'

'This really isn't the time or the place, Isy.'

'It never is with you, though, is it? I trusted you with my heart,' she said with more honesty than she'd intended, 'and you broke it. And you still won't tell me the truth.'

Not daring to say another word, she handed him her half-finished cup of coffee. She watched as he finished it, as he'd done so many times before, before turning to move away. Pain pricking its way forwards, as it always did, against a wound which refused to heal. The realisation that love didn't conquer all. That it didn't stand a chance, not when there were secrets and lies, and a story half told.

Chapter 5

The following morning, Isy had everything neatly packed away. The emotions, hope, and reality, were all perfectly compartmentalised, pushed back into the past where they belonged. It was the present that was causing her slightly more concern. Two men dressed in white were standing at the foot of her bed, staring down at her polka-dot pyjamas with very polite grins on their faces.

And for a moment she thought she'd died and gone to heaven. Then Jack arrived and she realised just how mistaken she was.

'Can no one read?' she asked in desperation. 'Or is this open house season? There's a very big sign on my door, saying *Keep Out!*'

'They're Polish. And no, they can't read, at least not English.'

'Oh,' she said, feeling herself blush a perfect shade of pink. 'I'm so sorry,' she muttered in her best attempt at the language.

Jack narrowed his gaze. 'Since when have you become bilingual?'

'My PA is from Poland. She keeps apologising to her husband. Why do they keep looking at me like that?'

'Possibly because your pyjama top isn't buttoned up properly and there's slightly more…'

But before he could finish, she'd grabbed the item by the lapels. 'There,' she said, making a shooing action with her other hand towards the two Poles, 'peep show over – now back to work!'

Jack made an apologetic gesture of his own as Wiktor and Jakub beat a hasty retreat. 'I indicated they could start stripping where they wanted, and I guess they chose you. Yours. The wallpaper,' he added in case there was any doubt, but she knew exactly what he meant. She also knew that his eyes had been admiring her breast too, and the thought made her heart flutter slightly faster than was acceptable.

'I'm going back to London,' she said, as he went to follow them out.

'London?' he queried, turning around to face her. It was obvious that this was the last thing he expected her to say. 'So soon?'

'I think it's better this way.'

'And,' he asked slowly, 'will you be coming back?'

She wanted to say no. She wanted to punish him for yesterday, for today, for everything she was feeling. The confusion and the lies, for still not being trusted with the truth, but she couldn't.

'If this is about what happened at the hospital,' he began. 'I'm sorry if you felt I wasn't being honest, but it was too open, too public. If you want to know about Jess, about the business, why don't you call round and see her? She's renting one of your father's cottages. I'm sure she'll be only too happy to see you and tell you what we're doing, herself.'

Isy put her hand out in protest, dropping her lapels, before quickly retrieving them. The last thing she wanted to see was their cosy love nest. 'No, no, no,' she said before the image took hold. 'There's no need. I'm going back to London because I need to see Tom. I need to explain to him, face to face, what I'm proposing. And then I need to go and see the senior partner of my firm, to find out if he'll agree to me working down here, on a part time basis, for a few months. If not, I'll have to think again…'

'Isy?'

'Yes?'

'You will phone me, won't you, if you change your mind?'

She looked at him confused. 'About what?'

'About coming back?'

And suddenly it took all her strength not to stand up and hurl herself at him, from the end of her bed. To wipe away the look of self-doubt she could see flash across his face. *Tom,* she told herself sternly. *Think of Tom.*

'Yes,' she said slowly. 'Of course, I'll tell you. Just in case I change my mind.'

'You're quiet tonight, my lad,' Frank said, as Jack stared down at the iPhone in his hand. 'And checking that constantly isn't going to bring her back any sooner.'

Jack knew that. Of course, he knew that and part of him wished the damned thing hadn't been invented. Only he was waiting for a text that hadn't come. A WhatsApp message to tell him she'd left and was on her way home.

'It's almost seven o'clock,' Frank said, checking his watch. 'Why don't you try to phone her and tell her to wait until tomorrow? Then you can go out with your mates, and I won't have to worry about her driving back in the dark?'

'I tried,' he said, trying to shrug it off, as though it was of no consequence. 'She didn't pick up.'

'You've got to stop doing this, you know,' Frank said, leaning towards him. 'You've got to let her go. You did it before. You can do it again.'

Jack wasn't so sure. She'd been gone two days now and it seemed like forever. 'I should have told her everything before she left for London the first time. *We* should have told her everything when you took me in.'

'She was too young. She wouldn't have understood.'

Well, she sure as hell isn't going to understand now, he wanted to say, to rid himself of some of the frustration he was feeling. She'd think he'd lied to her again, and she'd be right.

'Look,' Frank began quietly, 'there's no need for her to know, unless you change your mind about how you want to deal with it. In fact, I think it's probably best she doesn't, because I know my daughter. She's like her mother. She'll tell us exactly what she thinks about us and then try to put it right. And she can't.'

Jack didn't need Frank to tell him that. He'd learnt it from the tender age of five when the police had arrived on his doorstep with a message of their own.

'Go home, my lad,' Frank said, as though he knew where Jack was. 'Take the night off. You deserve it. You more than deserve it. Just make sure you leave a couple of lights on, as you know how much she hates coming back to the dark.'

*

It was the first thing Isy saw as she edged the car cautiously along the drive. A cavalcade of illumination drawing her home, and she was grateful for it. She'd never intended to stay an extra day in London, but Tom had wanted to celebrate his success. Then tell her exactly what he thought of her three-month secondment to the back of beyond.

'And what about us, Bella?' he'd asked, as she'd tried to reassure him. 'What about you and me?'

'What about you and me?' she asked, not quite sure what he meant. 'I'm not deserting you, you know,' she added, wondering why he thought she was. 'I'll still be coming back in between.'

Tom didn't look convinced. 'I'll miss you,' he said, as they set off for work the following morning. 'It won't be the same.'

'Of course, it will. You'll hardly notice I'm gone. You're back late most nights, anyway. And it's not as though you rely on me for domestics. You've already got someone who does that. All you've got to do is master the washing machine and the microwave, and you'll be fine.'

'I'll eat out,' he said stubbornly.

'Then you'll put on weight and you know how you hate that.' She paused as they reached the entrance to the train station. 'Look, I'm going back down tonight, my darling, and I'd like to leave knowing you don't hate me for it? That we can make this work?'

Then, when he didn't answer and she could sense his confusion, she leapt up and gave him a kiss on the lips. 'You can be such a creature of habit at times, but I guess that's boarding school for you, so you're forgiven.'

His features finally relaxed. 'I suppose I could always come and visit at the weekends.'

'Only don't bring the Porsche,' she said, with a sigh of relief. 'And go and buy some overalls as Jack will get you to do something, knowing him, and you won't want to borrow his, trust me. You have no idea where they've been.'

It was a comforting thought, Jack and his overalls. A thought that only a week ago, she'd have purged from her mind before it could take root. And Isy hated it, that after six years of denial, she could no longer simply block out Jack's existence by burying herself in London with Tom. A man who was proving to be just as elusive as Jack.

'Don't like goodbyes, you know that, Bella,' he'd said, when she'd finally tracked him down at his office. 'Never have. Much better you just go and text me when you're there.'

She wasn't best impressed. Were all men emotionally bankrupt, she began to wonder, if she discounted her father? Control freaks – manipulating her with the use of modern technology? Jack had said to WhatsApp him when she left; now Tom was saying to text him when she arrived. Flinging her iPhone into the depths of her handbag, she'd decided, she'd do neither.

Instead she'd congratulate herself on her success today. How she'd managed to persuade her firm she could go part-time and satisfy their needs with careful coordination and excellent communication.

'Capital,' the senior partner had told her, when she'd laid out her plan. 'Millie's coming back from maternity leave. You can job share with her. Excellent idea. Do you fancy a drink?'

She hadn't. She'd dressed to impress in a tailored suit, with her hair braided in a plait to the back, her feet slipped into heels that tilted everything she possessed to maximum effect. But that didn't mean she wanted to be another notch on his bedstead.

'Thanks so much,' she'd said, as appreciatively as she could, 'perhaps another time? I have so much to do. You do understand, don't you?' And with the perfect smile of promises to come, she'd turned her back on her employer, whose piercing eyes she could still feel undressing her, long after she'd left the chaos of London behind.

'Jack?' Isy called out quietly, as she went from room to room, turning out the lights. It was after two in the morning and she didn't expect him to be awake, but there was a glow coming from the study, a light not usually left on. And so, wondering if he was still up, burning the midnight oil, she wandered through the silence, to find him asleep, slumped in her father's favourite armchair.

There were, indeed, papers before him, sprawled across the footstool, but she guessed he'd not spent the whole of the evening studying them. He'd been out. She could tell by the clothes he was wearing. The aroma of alcohol wafting gently towards her. The way he'd placed his wallet next to his mobile.

'Just to check I've still got it,' he'd once said, a little the worse for wear.

And she knew she ought to walk away and leave him. That it made no sense to stay. Only he looked so appealing just lying there in the half-light, with his legs outstretched, his shirt buttons partially undone, that all she wanted to do was snuggle down beside him. A feeling so precious, so overwhelming, she could have cried if she'd thought it would have done any good.

Instead, she crept back outside, and retrieved her mobile from her bag. She glanced down at his text. At the WhatsApp message sealed with a kiss. Guilt eating away at her, as she returned to the study and tapped out a response of her own. She pressed send. The ping broke the silence. His head shot up, but he didn't see her standing there, watching him. It was only when he'd read the words *I'm here*, that he looked up, his bloodshot eyes adjusting to the light, just before he smiled; that long, lascivious smile she'd missed so much.

'Hello,' she said quietly, as he stretched out his arm towards her, his palm open, waiting for her to respond and show him she cared.

'I missed you,' he said thickly. 'You know that, don't you?'

She did, and she knew she should reject him as succinctly as he'd rejected her all those years ago. Only she couldn't. Not now. Not once she'd felt the pressure of his grip against hers, the warmth of his reception, drawing her closer and closer, until there was nowhere left for her to go.

'We'll speak in the morning,' she managed to say, as she saw the passion ignite in his eyes. But before she could respond, or even begin to douse the flames, he raised her fingers to his lips and kissed them, with the gentlest, the most provocative of touches.

And she cursed herself for her naivety. Her stupidity in thinking she could handle this, because she couldn't. She was so out of her depth, she couldn't even see the shore, let alone swim to it. So, with a firm but reluctant tug, she retrieved her hand from his grasp and forced herself to move away, her heart betraying her future with every step she took.

'Until tomorrow,' she heard herself say. But she wasn't listening, at least, not to herself. She was too busy thinking of Tom. The man she still had to text, to tell him everything was fine. And then, when she'd done that, when she'd finally gathered her wits about her, she had to try to convince herself too.

Jack leant back in Frank's chair and stared at the empty doorway. His mind, though, was elsewhere. His thoughts spiralling back in time to the evening of her twenty-first birthday. When she'd stared up at him, in a nightclub in Exeter, and asked him the one question he knew he mustn't answer.

'Do you find me attractive?'

She was studying him with those large green eyes. Her body demanding his attention, as only hers ever could; dressed to impress in a tightly fitting slip of material, that wrapped itself seductively around her curves. Whilst the lights in the club flashed off and on, with a kaleidoscope of colours in between.

And he knew he should ignore her. That he should smother his thoughts with another drink, but it was a little late for that. He was on his fourth beer, and she was still as beautiful as she'd been during his first. But he couldn't tell her that. He couldn't tell her he fancied her like hell. That he'd been dreaming of this moment ever since she'd begged him to be her very own Romeo. He owed it to Frank, his godfather, to exercise restraint, and exercise restraint he would.

But it was hard, bloody hard, when she looked at him like that, with that heady mix of hope and trust. And, for the first time since he'd felt the pangs of pain, of unrequited love, he began to wonder, if maybe she felt it too? That it hadn't been his imagination back in Sheffield. Or some sort of drunken dare dreamt up by her and Jess to see how far he'd go when push came to shove.

'How much have you had to drink?' he heard himself ask, against a tidal wave of drum and base.

'Two glasses of wine,' she shouted back at him, against the beat. 'You see, I'm perfectly sober,' she added, coming towards him, leaving her friends in the background. 'Probably more sober than you are. So,' she asked again, staring straight up at him. 'Do you think I'm attractive?'

He could feel his mates move away, merging into the crowd, and he knew he should do the same, before it was too late, from the one woman who was exciting every nerve cell he had and a few more besides.

'Attractive?' he queried, flinging the word back to her as he tried to focus on the question and not her proximity. 'You know you're attractive.'

'That's not what I said.'

'Isy...'

'Yes?'

'I really don't think we should be having this conversation.'

'And why not?'

'Because...because...'

'Because you *do* find me attractive, don't you?' A smile of triumph spread across her face. 'Jess was right.'

'I never said that.'

'You don't have to. You see, Jack, I know exactly what you're thinking,' she murmured, bringing her lips up to his and kissing him softly, seducing his senses while he struggled for restraint. 'I know you want to kiss me back,' she whispered in his ear, her breath sweet and warm, 'but you're scared. And I don't want you to be scared, because I'm not.'

His eyes darted across to where Jess was standing, and he wondered what the hell he'd said or done that could have led her to this conclusion, to infiltrate his innermost desires, because it was wrong, so wrong, but yet it felt so right. So bloody right, because he *did* want to kiss Isy back. He wanted to do exactly what she wanted and more. So much more, that he felt himself respond at just the mere thought of it.

She'd been his salvation back then, goddamn it. The panacea for all his ills, and for a few careless months he'd thought he was hers, foolish romantic that he was. He'd dared to dream; he'd said 'yes' when he should have said 'no'. He'd held her close when he should have let her go. He'd done everything he knew he shouldn't, and by God he'd paid the price.

The only question now, as he finally closed his eyes, was how the hell was he going to stop himself from making the same mistake again? To find a way to make amends, yet set her free? When every nerve in his body wanted her to stay – with him, and only him?

Chapter 6

Isy knew exactly what she was going to do. She was going to try once again to forget Jack ever existed. Only she knew it wouldn't be easy, because it never was. He was always there, somewhere, infiltrating her dreams, however hard she tried to keep him out, and tonight was no exception. Before she knew it, she was back in his bed, cuddling up to him, as though she'd never been away.

'So, was it good for you?' she heard herself ask. A little purr of delight caught in her throat, while she waited for him to respond. To say something that mirrored her thoughts, because last night, at her twenty-first, had been more than good for her. It had been ecstatic from the moment he'd finally cracked and kissed her. In front of everyone!

And now she'd awoken to a new day. A new life. A perfect summer's morning, with sunlight streaming through the curtains and she wanted him to stir and tell her she wasn't hallucinating. That he'd meant every word he'd said, and more, as he'd sent her spiralling out of this world, to the galaxies and the universe beyond.

'Jack?' she murmured, wriggling round in his arms to face him. 'You *are* awake.'

'No good asking me questions if I'm not,' he teased, raising her fingers to his lips and kissing them tenderly.

'So,' she managed to gasp, '*was* it good for you?'

'Do you need to ask?'

But before she could reply and ask for a little more clarification, he'd raised himself up onto his elbow, and was gazing down at her with so much desire, that all she wanted to do was throw herself at him, and ask him to do it all over again.

'Thank you,' she said softly, with a sigh of complete satisfaction, 'for the best birthday present ever.' Stretching up, she gave him the gentlest of kisses on his lips before collapsing back against the sheets to enjoy the view. His body, so toned and tempting, was so tantalisingly close she couldn't resist stretching out and touching it, her fingers playing with the fine sprinkling of hairs as they traced a path gently, caressingly, towards his hips. 'Why,' she murmured, 'did we never do this before?'

'Because, my darling, you never asked me.'

But she couldn't respond. She couldn't tell him what a fool she'd been, because he was pressing his lips gently against hers, and she needed all her breath to kiss him back.

'You're so…so…' he groaned, breaking off.

Provocative? Beautiful? Demanding? She didn't care which adjective he used, just as long as he didn't stop. Only nothing was happening as it should. She could hear Jack's voice calling her, but the tone had changed. It was becoming more and more insistent, and his fingers weren't where they should be, playing with her to perfection. They were pressing down on her shoulders.

And suddenly she realised she wasn't dreaming. She was half awake and Jack was there in the room beside her, the force of his presence invading her space, as he tried to bring her back from wherever it was she'd been.

'For Christ's sake, Isy, wake up.' His breath was warm against her cheeks. 'I need to speak to you.'

In total panic, she opened her eyes. 'Jack,' she gasped, frantically crossing her legs, to quell her frustration. 'What the hell do you think you're doing here?' she asked, trying desperately to find him in the dark.

'Listening to you murmuring sweet nothings to Tom.' Only he didn't sound amused. 'It's your father…'

'My father?' She struggled to sit up, as he pulled away. 'What about my father?'

'The hospital called. He's got further chest pain, so they've taken him back to theatre to check what's happening. Whether it's cardiac in origin or not. Again, nothing to worry about, but he wanted them to let us know.'

Nothing to worry about? 'Would people please stop telling me there's nothing to worry about when it's perfectly clear that there is!' She flung off the covers as Jack threw her a jumper.

'I'm going to have a quick shower,' he said, 'then we can drive over. Or, rather, you'll have to. I'm still over the limit. Unless you want to go without me?'

She had no intention of going anywhere without him. Or with him. She was far more preoccupied with trying to find her slippers. Her sheepskin filled saviours. Although why she was worrying about them and how to put her jumper on over her pyjamas, made absolutely no sense as she wasn't going to the hospital in her night clothes.

'What's the time?' she asked, grabbing her clock, to see it was five thirty. 'He will be all right, won't he?' she called out to Jack, as he paused in the doorway.

'Of course, he will,' he said, in that way he had of dismissing uncertainty. But she knew, as he disappeared, that he had no more idea than she did. That the room was strangely empty without him. And she really must concentrate on getting dressed.

Jack was throwing all his efforts into clarity of thought and rehydration. 'Here you go,' he said, passing Isy a pack of biscuits and a beaker of coffee. 'Breakfast,' he added, as he sat back down opposite her in the waiting room and opened yet another bottle of water for himself. Driving across country with Isy at the wheel was not the best way to sober up, but there was absolutely no way he was leaving her to face this by herself.

'Feeling better?' she asked, as he opened his third sausage roll.

He gave her the briefest of nods. 'Only next time when I say stop at a crossroads, do you think you could do that before we go across it? Emergency braking, not such a great idea.'

'Better than crashing into something,' she said with a confidence he didn't entirely share. His attention, though, was diverted as a nurse appeared in the doorway.

'Ms Forrester? Dr Choudhary would like to see you now.'

They both stood up.

'And you are?' the nurse asked him. And for a moment he

hesitated, as though weighing up the best way to define himself, or his presence here.

'Jack's family,' Isy said before he could. 'My father's adopted son.'

It was the first time she'd called him that and he wasn't sure how he felt about it. He was no longer the brother she'd never had, or the lover she'd adored. And it reminded him of a time long gone, when she'd first tackled the question of his heritage. Only then her response had been a little more inclusive.

'You need the structure, my lad, the discipline,' Frank had said, when he'd sent Jack off to the same private school as Isy. 'It will be the making of you.'

It wasn't. He hated it. The fact that he had to travel home with a six-year-old didn't help. It was like being on a game show where the questions never stopped.

'Did you remember your homework? What did you have for lunch? Did you know that Jess got hit by Cassie Malone? I don't like her, do you?'

He didn't know who the fuck Cassie Malone was and at that time he didn't give a shit. He was slightly intrigued by the fact that Isy never gave up. It didn't matter how monosyllabic he was, or how much he'd ignored her on the bus going home, she would still want to be his friend. This devotion to a lost cause was new to him and it made him think that maybe he wasn't quite as lost as he'd always thought. Bit by bit, and month by month, he began to warm to her and when Cassie Malone started on her, he made bloody sure he knew all about her and that Cassie never did it again.

By the time Christmas arrived, three months later, he'd got used to Isy's endearing little ways. He was also looking forward to the first proper Christmas of his life.

'We have a tree. A real one. Dad puts it up in the hall and I help him decorate. Only last year, it almost fell over.'

'That's because you tried to climb it to put the fairy back,' Frank explained. They were sitting in his study. Jack was trying to master algebra, and Isy a glitter pen which wouldn't work. And he'd never felt happier or more at home in his life.

Then Isy looked up at him from where she'd been sitting on the floor and fired the first of a volley of shots he'd have done anything to avoid.

'Why aren't you going home for Christmas? Don't you want to see your mummy and daddy? Do you know what they're getting you for a present?'

'Isabella, I think it's time you went and asked Mrs White for your tea, don't you, my dear?'

It was obvious she didn't. 'Won't they miss you?' she asked, as Jack got up to do what Frank had suggested.

'Isy,' her father said quickly, a warning note in his voice, but it was too late. Isy was following Jack through the drawing room and out in the hall.

'Don't they love you?' she asked, as her father joined them.

'No, they bloody well don't,' Jack replied before Frank could. 'They're bloody dead. And you should mind your own bloody business.'

As soon as he'd opened his mouth, he regretted it. The shock in her eyes, in the innocence he no longer had, would haunt him for the rest of his life. It still did, but then, twenty years ago, anger was his only line of defence.

'Let's go and see Mrs White for our tea,' her father said kindly, with a warning gesture to Jack to leave them alone for a few minutes, so he could try to comfort his daughter. But it was soon clear to both of them that Isy didn't need comforting. Not once she'd digested the information. Instead, she went up to where Jack was standing and took him by the hand and led him to the kitchen.

'Mrs White,' she said pointedly, 'Jack needs cake because his parents are dead.'

Jack could see the housekeeper look at Frank and then back at Isy. He then watched as Mrs White placed a large slab of Victoria sandwich on a plate for Isy to present to him.

'My mother's dead too,' she said with a solemnity that far outweighed her years. 'But you can have my father. We can share him,' she added, beaming up at him. 'And when you've finished your cake, you can write to Santa Claus and then you'll get lots and lot of presents. Like me!'

The smile she gave him made Jack want to cry. It still did, all these years later. He wanted to reach out and touch the woman beside him. To say he knew how it felt, to be on the outside looking in, waiting for a stranger to give you the news that could change the rest of your life.

'So, he's going to be all right, my father?' she was asking as he forced himself to stay where he was. 'You had to put another stent in but he's going to be OK?'

'I cannot give you any guarantees,' the doctor replied, a small man with a turban and a welcoming air of confidence. 'He's had high blood pressure for years, as you know. He needs to start taking his condition seriously. To exercise but not overdo it, to cut out on stress, and then we'll see.'

'Stress – cut out on stress? How can he cut out on stress?' Isy bemoaned. 'We're turning the Hall into a wedding venue!'

Jack liked the use of *we,* but that was about the only thing he liked. He was as out of the loop on Frank's health as Isy and it didn't make him feel particularly good about himself. He wanted to comfort her, too, to say something reassuring, but platitudes didn't seem appropriate. And even if they were, he wasn't sure she would accept them. He'd crossed a line last night, when he'd kissed her hand. A stupid bloody line in the sand and now he needed to redraw it, for the sake of his sanity as well as hers.

She glanced up at him, her eyes awash with tears. 'Did you know about any of this?' she asked when they were alone. 'That Dad had heart problems?'

He shook his head although he could tell she wasn't convinced, that she'd probably never believe anything he said ever again.

'I want to believe you,' she admitted as though she could read his mind, 'but the pair of you are as thick as thieves sometimes, and I no longer know what to think.'

'Then don't, just accept.'

'That my father could die?'

'He won't, Isy. Not yet. It's not his time.'

'And you know that, do you? The man who lied to me about his own parents. What gives you the right to talk to me about mine?'

But before he could counter her accusation with some form

of mediation, she'd gone, leaving the room with its revelations behind her.

He didn't try to catch up with her. She was hurting and she needed her space. He accepted that. Instead, he followed at a discreet distance. It was only when she reached the car park, and turned to see where he was, that he quickened his stride. 'I assume you don't want to see your father?'

'I can't,' she said, brushing away tears with the back of her hand. 'Not now. Not like this.' She glanced up at him and gave him a dignified sniff. 'Did you know?'

'No, of course I didn't. Do you think I would have let him do what he's been doing for the last few years, if I had? Do you really think I'm that shallow, that much of a bastard, after everything he's done for me?'

He waited while she studied him. Those large green eyes seeking his for some sign of unity that this was a pain they could share as equals, and not as adversaries.

'I believe you,' she said finally.

'Thank God for that. Now, unless you're planning to ban me from the car, may I suggest we go home? You get some rest. I'll attack the landscaping again and we'll come back and see your father this afternoon. And Isy...'

'Yes?'

'He *is* going to be all right.'

That Jack could have so much certainty puzzled her, but Isy was grateful for the reassurance. She couldn't rest, though. How could she? When every time she closed her eyes, she saw her father?

So, instead, she found the oldest pair of trousers and T-shirt she owned, stuffed at the back of a drawer, and set off to help Jack.

The sun was surprisingly hot for the end of September. A flurry of wasps hovered over some late flowering hibiscus, while the beauty of the sea flashed at her through the trees. It was a moment of peace in a troubled world and she was grateful for it. Only something was missing. Some semblance of noise. It was just too quiet.

So, she set off to investigate, jogging down the drive, until she came to the turning she'd discovered on her first night back. A freshly dug route, filled with gravel, stretched out before her, ready to take their guests around the perimeter of the grounds, but there was no Jack. No ex-lover in filthy overalls, to congratulate. Just a mini excavator glistening in the midday sun, looking as lonely as she felt.

Where are you? she wondered, retrieving her mobile from her trouser pocket. She pressed his number. Only it went straight to voicemail. She waited a few minutes, then tried again. Still no response, which could mean so many things, but she was too tired to try to work out which. All she knew was that he wasn't where he'd said he'd be, which meant he had to be somewhere else.

'Go to him, Isy,' Jess had begged her, on the night of her twenty-first birthday. 'Go to Jack. He's crazy about you.'

'Don't be so silly,' she'd replied, trying to dismiss the thought before it could take hold. 'He's going out with you.'

'No, no, he's not. I wish he was, but he's not.'

She stared at Jess's sad reflection in the cloakroom mirror. 'But I thought, after the concert… After he took you to see Muse?'

Jess shook her head. 'He's just a friend, a very good friend, but it's you he wants, Isy. I can see it in his eyes when he thinks no one's looking. He loves you, you idiot, he just doesn't know how to tell you.'

Isy stared at the two cottages in front of her. Once dilapidated, her father had renovated them a few years ago for his labourers. Now one of them housed her oldest school friend, whom she'd kept in touch with via Facebook but very little else.

What a difference six years makes, she thought. *Now Jack's in love with you and it's my turn to try to be brave.* She peered in through the windows. The first cottage had a vase of fresh flowers and Laura Ashley curtains, while the second had an array of empty beer cans.

She chose the first. Picking up the knocker, she took a deep breath, fixed a happy smile on her face and waited. Only no one came. And she was just about to walk away when the door creaked open and Jess appeared.

'Isy,' she said, looking a little flustered but not at all surprised to see her, 'I'm so sorry about your father.'

Isy felt her smile falter. 'He's going to be all right,' she said, before hugging her oldest friend hello. 'I'm so sorry that I've not been round before, that I've left it for so long, but I don't suppose you've seen Jack, have you?' she asked, following Jess inside, into a room of blues and creams, and a log burner that looked as though it might actually work. 'Only he's not exactly where he said he was going to be.'

'And you,' Jack interrupted, 'aren't exactly where you said you were going to be.' Isy watched as he came down the stairs towards her, her eyes drifting towards the lower part of his body and then back up again at his face.

'It's all fixed now,' he said, ignoring Isy completely, which left her wondering what he could be referring to.

'Was something broken?' she asked in feigned innocence.

And she could tell he wanted to burst out laughing and come back at her with a quip of his own, but he couldn't, not in front of Jess.

'Look, if I've interrupted something here,' she said, as casually as she could, 'I'm sorry. I just wanted to check that you're OK.'

'And why wouldn't I be?'

She glanced up at him, at the amused tilt of his brow. 'Because…'

'Yes?'

'Would you like a coffee?' Jess interrupted, coming to her rescue, as she'd done so many times before. Her whole countenance just as Isy remembered it to be, an English rose without the thorns, and she could see why Jack would fall in love with her. She was just surprised it had taken him so long.

'Another time, maybe?' *When he's not here*, she wanted to add. *When I can pretend he never was?*

'I'll walk back with you.' Jack's voice captured her thoughts. Yet, before she could resist and tell him exactly what he could do with them, he'd retrieved his jacket from the back of the sofa and was giving Jess a kiss goodbye. 'Everything should be working fine,' he told her. 'Any problems, just let me know.'

And Isy knew she shouldn't ask. That it was really none of her business. That she should discuss the weather, or at least the price of eggs, but she couldn't.

'What's working now?' she asked, as they walked across the grass.

'Wouldn't you like to know?'

'Absolutely not. If you don't want to tell me… Only if you do…'

'I don't…'

'I know, but in case you do…'

'You haven't changed, do you know that?'

'I'm going to take that as a compliment.'

'You can take it any way you wish but I'm still not going to tell you.'

'Are you having sex with Jess?' It was out before she could stop herself, and one glance at him made her wish she'd tried just that bit harder. He'd come to a halt, as though they were both teetering at the edge of a tornado, rather than the side of a digger called Fred.

'Are you having sex with Tom?' he asked, swinging round to face her.

'Of course, I am,' she answered without hesitation. 'We're going out.'

'So, if I'm going out with Jess, it would be OK with you for me to have sex with her?'

'Of course, it would,' she lied.

'And you wouldn't mind in the slightest?'

She shook her head, her heart pounding at the deceit. 'Why, should I?'

He didn't answer. He just stared at her and she could tell he was as confused as she was. That he was sifting through a retinue of responses, trying to work out which one to use. And when he didn't, when he turned away and walked back towards Jess's cottage, it was the worst response of all.

Chapter 7

'Bella, I'm thinking of coming down to Devon next weekend. What do you say?'

Isy could hear the noise of the bar behind Tom, the clinking of glasses and people talking over each other. It was almost as deafening as the silence of the Hall.

'Wonderful.'

'It is, isn't it? Henry and Tricia are sailing off Dartmouth. They've got a yacht down there. Said we might join them.'

She wasn't entirely sure that Tom had quite grasped the concept of *help* here. That sipping champagne on a crew-provided vessel didn't really qualify, but she didn't pursue it. She'd spent the whole evening, following her trip to the cottage, trying to keep herself busy. Removing pictures from the walls in the drawing room, then packing away anything that was remotely breakable ahead of Wiktor's and Jakub's return tomorrow.

By the time Jack came back, she could hardly stand let alone conduct a coherent conversation. So, she collapsed down onto the sofa and waited for him to join her.

'I'm in here,' she yelled out, to give him a clue. 'Unless, of course, you're a burglar, then I'm a hologram.'

'I sincerely hope not,' he confided, joining her in the drawing room. 'One of you is more than enough, even on a good day.'

She opened her mouth to protest but then she noticed where he was heading. 'If you're looking for the decanters, they're in the box marked exhibit A, along with the bottles of whisky.' She paused. 'You didn't come to the hospital this afternoon?' she asked, hoping he was no longer cross with her.

'I went tonight.' He looked up from rescuing his supply of alcohol from the box. 'Any particular reason why you packed these away?'

'Just in case our strippers were tempted.'

'So, you were hiding it from them and not from me?'

She looked at him puzzled. He seemed strangely affected by what she'd done, and she had absolutely no idea why. 'You told me to pack everything that was either breakable or precious away to protect it. The decanters were my grandfather's and the whisky is expensive.'

He retrieved a couple of glasses from the wrapping and offered her one.

She shook her head. 'I've had my hot chocolate,' she said, indicating the empty mug on the table before her. 'Although I was surprised to find Dad had still kept the tin.'

'He never gave up hope.'

'That I'd come back?' She watched him closely as he poured himself a drink and sank down on the sofa opposite. 'Did you think I'd come back?'

'What do you think?' His voice was light, but she knew his response wasn't.

That I'd stay away? That I'd do as I'd promised? That you'd never have to see me again? Her thoughts ran riot in her mind. Only, when she looked across at him, she realised that wasn't where they'd stayed.

'If you're fishing for compliments,' he informed her dryly, 'I think you're going to need a bigger net.'

'How big?'

'Trawler sized.'

'That's not entirely fair,' she began, before conceding he was probably right. 'I think I should go to bed.' But she couldn't leave. Not until she'd done the one thing she'd been promising herself she'd do all evening. 'I'm sorry,' she said, before she could change her mind, 'for what I said outside Jess's, I really am. If you're happy with her, then I'm glad.' And to prove it, she pulled herself up off the sofa and went over to where he was sitting.

'Friends?' she asked, hoping he'd agree. Then, bending over, she gave his cheek the lightest of kisses goodnight. Only this time, he didn't kiss her back. This time he didn't say anything. He just stared back up at her with a look she knew only too well. And she knew she was in trouble, before she even had a chance to straighten up.

You still love me, she thought, in utter desperation. *You still want me, even though you know you shouldn't. That it's hopeless.* And what made it worse, a hundred times worse, was the fact that he wasn't alone, because she wanted him too. She wanted to reach out and touch him, to kiss him, and to hold him; to do all the things they used to do together.

And she wished with all her heart it wasn't so. For Tom's sake.

For Jess's sake, let alone their own. She wished she could find a way to expel the past, and keep those ghosts at bay, but she couldn't. Not now she was back in Devon and there were less than 200 miles between them. Between her and the man who was looking at her as though he knew exactly what she was thinking.

Chapter 8

'This isn't good.' Isy glanced up at Jack apprehensively and then away as quickly as she could. Her attention centered on the large gap in the drawing-room wall, while Wiktor and Jakub hovered in the background, speaking to each other in animated Polish.

'I suspect they're saying it's not their fault,' she offered. And, in fairness, it probably wasn't. She knew, as any child of a builder knew, that accidents happened. That pipes broke. Wires snapped. And large chunks of plaster sometimes came off walls, especially when the construction wasn't that sound in the first place.

'I suppose we should be grateful it's not happened before.'

Jack didn't look so convinced. 'The trouble with Georgian buildings, is that they weren't always built by the best craftsmen,' he said, feeling the crumbling brick behind. 'Or rather the outer walls were but the inner walls were often built by their apprentices.'

She could remember her father telling her this, that the levels often didn't tie up, that there was no bonding, or the gaps were stuffed with rubbish, which didn't help.

'Solution?' she asked optimistically.

'See what happens when they remove the rest of the paper.'

'And?'

'Pray that we don't need to fund anything from the contingency fund, because there isn't one.'

'If that's meant to reassure me, I've got news for you – it doesn't!'

In fact, nothing Jack had said or done since that night in the drawing room had reassured her. She'd spent the last few days trying to avoid him. It hadn't been hard. There was so much to do, trying to set up a satellite office of Havers and Co. Not to mention trying to put in place plans for her father's imminent discharge.

Only now her presence was required, especially as Wiktor had sought her out in the first place. 'OK, let's forget about the contingency fund,' she began tentatively, 'because it appears there isn't one. I suppose we'll have to let the conservation officer know, though, to try to keep her happy?'

Jack moved a little closer. 'Are you implying that I'm not – keeping the lady happy?'

'No. No. Of course not. Only…' Only the words wouldn't come. How could they when he was standing within kissing distance? All thoughts of Wiktor and Jakub banished to a distant hemisphere when she glanced up and saw the proximity of those lips.

'You're right,' she said in a frantic attempt to get back to what they were talking about before she'd introduced conservation officers and confusion. 'We should stick to the truth. About the restoration,' she added in case he had any doubts. 'And Dad.'

'But not about us?'

'I know the truth about us, Jack. I know the truth about you.'

He raised an eyebrow, but it wasn't done in acknowledgement.

It was a fleeting, almost subconscious, rejection of what she'd said, and she knew she should ask him exactly what he meant, but he never gave her a chance. Without another word being spoken, he was gone, leaving her with the strangest sense of déjà vu.

It had been a perfect September evening; however hard Isy tried to rewrite history, in the years that followed, she couldn't dismiss that. The sun was languishing peacefully overhead when they lay down together for the very last time, their bodies soaking up its rays from their rugs on the sand. While towering red cliffs sheltered them from a gentle breeze which was drifting its way aimlessly around the cove.

It was the moment she'd been waiting for all day. The moment when she'd tell Jack about her brilliant idea for their future and hope he'd agree. Only, first, she needed to concentrate on something a little closer to home.

'I could spend every waking moment of my life with you,' he declared, trailing his fingers teasingly against her flesh, 'and never get bored.'

'Me too,' she murmured, as she felt herself begin to respond, 'I mean with you.'

He smiled. 'You know what I want to do to you, don't you?'

She did and the thought of it caused a chorus of delight to burst forth from within. 'I don't think we should,' she said, with a giggle she couldn't suppress.

'And why's that, my darling?' His hand drifting closer and closer towards her bikini briefs. 'Because I know you want to, and I know,' he added huskily, 'that all I need to do is touch you here...'

'And I'll never let you stop.' She squinted up at him, against the light, at the desire in his eyes, the warmth in his smile as he drew her towards him. His legs, his shorts, his arousal, all so close, so firm against her thighs. 'Only...'

'Only what?'

'Only what if someone sees us? I...I don't want to be arrested for...for lewd behaviour.'

'There is nothing lewd about you.' His face only inches from hers. 'Nothing lewd about you at all.'

And she hung on to that thought as he kissed her, and the world and its worries disappeared from view. It was only later, when he'd released her, when his tongue had teased and tantalised hers with a taste of what was to come, that she tried again.

'I'm going to be a...a solicitor...I have to be good.'

'And this isn't being good?' he queried thickly, 'because it feels bloody good to me.'

'You know what I mean.' She smiled up at him, her heart ranting at her to stop resisting, to lie back, and let him do what he did so well, to allow him access to every part of her body. But she couldn't. Not yet. 'I do love you, you know,' she assured him, her hands stroking the stubble on his cheeks. 'We're going to have such a great time in London.'

'London?' The word hung in the atmosphere, long after he'd repeated it. 'I thought you were going to ask for a transfer for your course? For your LPC?' he said, his eyes searching hers with an urgency she wasn't expecting. 'To Exeter?'

'I know. I know that's what we talked about. But would you mind terribly if we went to London?'

He looked as though he did, and she couldn't understand why. 'My mother trained as an artist in London,' she tried to explain. 'It would mean so much to me to train there too. As a solicitor.'

Still he didn't speak. And she begged him to agree with her, to stop acting as though he didn't, as though they were back on that school bus, and he didn't understand a word she was saying.

'What's the matter?' she asked, as he pulled himself away from her and sat up, his arms hanging loosely around his knees as he stared out to sea.

'I can't go to London,' he said finally.

'Why ever not? It's a lot closer than some of the places we were planning to visit, before I got my training contract. Besides, I'm sure Dad won't mind. He never expected us to stay with him, he's said that. Mrs White will continue to clean and take care of him, I know she will, if I ask.'

'It's not that simple.'

'Don't be silly. Of course, it is,' she said, sitting up beside him and slipping her dress over her bikini. 'You could get work in London. There must be loads of people who need building work done. You could specialise in carpentry or do a course. We could get a flat together. Dad will pay for the rent; he's already said he would.'

He turned to look at her. 'Did you tell him I was coming?'

She nodded.

'And he didn't say anything?'

'No, why should he?' She didn't add that he'd given her a funny look and asked if she was sure Jack had agreed to this, but he'd never pushed the point when she'd said she knew he would.

'You only suggested Exeter because you were worried about him. That's what you told me. Well, he's fine, so there's nothing to stop us. After all, you did say you'd show me the world.' She gave him the bravest of smiles, which faltered the moment he raised himself up off the rug and tugged his jeans back on over his shorts.

'I love you, Isy,' he declared. 'I love you so bloody much.'

'I know that,' she said, jumping up beside him.

'But I can't do it.'

She was beginning to get worried now. 'Are you saying that if I go to London, you won't come with me?'

He gave her a brief nod, his whole face racked with something she couldn't read, let alone understand.

'Why ever not?' she persisted, hoping he'd explain. 'What's wrong with London?' Then, when he didn't, when he started to move away towards the path which led back up to the Hall, she grabbed the rugs and followed. 'You're scaring me, Jack.'

He swung round and before she could say anything, he took hold of her arms with his hands, the rugs dropping to the ground between them. 'I'm asking you,' he said in a voice she scarcely recognised, 'to think again. To *please* think again.'

She gazed up at him as the sun started to descend. A brilliant shaft of light, orange and purple, cut through the gloom, but all she could see was the man she loved, and a black cloud about to burst over everything she thought she had.

'Is it to do with your parents?' she tried again. 'Is it because the memory is still too painful?'

His jaw tightened.

'Jack? Because if it is, we don't need to get a flat near where you used to live. London's huge. We can find somewhere different, where there are no memories.'

'It's not as easy as that.'

'Isn't it? Why isn't it?'

'Because,' he swallowed hard, 'because, damn you, my mother's not dead.'

She felt her jaw drop towards her toes. 'You mean she's alive?'

A ghost of a smile crossed his lips. 'I always knew you were bright.'

She didn't feel it. She felt as stupid as it was possible to feel. 'Does Dad know this?' But she knew the answer to that long before the words left her lips. Of course, her father would know. He was Jack's godfather. It was his duty to know these things.

She shook herself free. 'And when exactly were either of you planning to tell me?'

He didn't say anything. She could see the response in his eyes.

'Never. You were never planning to tell me this, were you?'

'It's not that simple.'

'Isn't it?'

'No, it isn't.'

'I don't agree, because if you loved me, it would be the simplest thing in the world.'

'It's because I love you... Because...' He stopped. She could see the anguish in his eyes, in every feature of that rugged face. 'Please, Isy, please don't make me explain.'

And part of her wanted to agree. She wanted to throw her arms around him, and tell him not to worry, that she understood, but she couldn't, because she didn't. She'd thought they were friends, the very best of friends long before they were lovers. Only right now, she was beginning to wonder if they were anything at all.

'I can't go to London,' he said, stepping back in despair, 'because if I do, I will need to see her, my mother. And I swore, all those years ago, that I couldn't…mustn't…that she was nothing to me.'

And why, she wanted to ask, *would your mother be nothing to you?* Only she knew what he'd say. She could see it in his eyes. That this was one question he couldn't answer, no matter how hard she tried. 'This isn't how it's meant to be, is it?' she gasped, reaching out and grabbing both of his hands in hers.

'Perhaps it never was?'

'You don't mean that.'

But he wasn't looking at her anymore. He was gazing down at her fingers, at the ring he'd bought her less than a week ago. 'It was a dream,' he said, the words almost choking him as he spoke. 'A beautiful bloody dream, but just a dream.' And with that, he withdrew his hands from hers and turned away.

'I don't believe you,' she said, as he bent over to scoop up the rugs from the sand. 'Jack are you listening to me? I said…'

'I know what you said.' He looked up and caught her gaze. She could tell he was listening, but he wasn't hearing a word she said. 'It's over, Isy. You. Me. Us. The whole bloody lot. You're better off without me.'

'Don't be so silly.' Only he didn't look as though he was joking. 'I don't want to be without you.'

'Then you're a fool.'

She fought back the tears. 'Why are you saying these things? Why are you being so cruel?'

He didn't speak. He was drowning, she could tell, and she knew she should throw him a lifeline as she'd done so many times before, but she couldn't. Not this time, because this time she was drowning too.

'Am I being punished?' she asked, frantically trying to make sense of it all. 'Is that what this is all about – for finding out about your mother?'

He clasped the rugs to his chest. 'I could never punish you, Isy. Never. I'm freeing you, that's what I'm doing.' His voice was taut with emotion. 'I'm letting you go.'

'Even if I don't want you to?'

'You will, trust me.'

She wasn't sure if she'd ever trust him again. All she knew was that she wanted to close her eyes and start the day again. To wake up in a world she recognised. Only what if nothing changed? If she found herself, once again, staring up at the only man she'd ever loved, as though her heart were about to break?

'I don't believe you,' she said, trying so hard to be brave. 'I will never believe you. But…but if you walk away from me now, I'll know that I'm wrong. That…that you really do mean it. That it's over. That I'm going to London alone.'

He hesitated. She was sure he hesitated. In the days, months, and years to come, she would go over those few seconds, time and time again. Searching for hope, when there was none to be had. Only grief, and a feeling of complete desolation as she watched Jack turn away from her, and head back towards the Hall.

She didn't follow him. It was all she could do to breathe, let alone walk. Instead, she collapsed down on their rock, their very special rock, and saw the sun go down on the day, on everything she'd ever hoped for or desired. Then, when she'd managed to compose herself a little, she forced herself back up onto her feet, and followed in his footsteps.

Her father was waiting for her on the porch. Jack, though, was nowhere to be seen.

'You must try to understand,' her father said, 'what it was like for him, leaving his home behind.'

Only she couldn't. All she could see was her future. A future without Jack. 'I'm going to go and stay with Auntie Beth before I go to London. I'm sorry, Dad, but I can't stay here, I just can't.'

'Then promise me you'll say goodbye, that you won't leave without saying goodbye to him?'

She stared up at him. At the man who'd known Jack's secret all along. 'Why didn't you tell me about his mother? Why didn't you let me know?'

'It was his story to tell, my dear, not mine. It was always for him to tell you, when he was ready.'

'Well, he's told me now,' she cried, before finally breaking down and throwing herself into her father's arms. 'And he doesn't want me anymore. And…and it hurts so much.'

'I know, my dear child, I know. And I suspect he's hurting too.'

'Do you? Do you really think so?' Only she wasn't so sure.

Her father didn't say another word. Nor did Jack when he finally returned, his face a sad reflection of the boy who'd arrived all those years ago. Only this time, she didn't take him by the hand and offer him her mother's pearl earrings. This time she turned her back on him, on the man she'd thought she knew. As she realised, for the very first time, she really didn't know him at all.

'You're looking a bit lost.' Jack's voice brought her back to the present. 'Why do I get the feeling you've not been listening to a word I've said?'

'Possibly because I've not?' she replied, watching as he reappeared from behind the Mini's open bonnet, his overalls stained with oil. 'Please don't hold it against me. It's just...'

'It's just what?'

'I've been remembering.'

He raised an eyebrow. 'Anything good?'

That there's something else you've not told me – that you're keeping from me? 'That I need to fill up with petrol. Is everything all right?' She tried to sound upbeat, but he didn't look convinced.

'If we're talking about the car,' he said, slamming the bonnet shut, 'then you should congratulate yourself, because you were right. It was the plugs and I've changed them.'

She allowed herself a mental hug. 'So, I can go and collect Dad from hospital and take him to my aunt's?'

He nodded. 'I've checked the tyres, too, and the water levels. It's good to go.'

She thanked him. She wasn't entirely useless under the bonnet herself, but she'd needed all the help she could get this morning, when the deal she was working on began to fall through. Tom, on the other hand, *was* hopeless. Present him with a mechanical problem and he'd sooner reach for his wallet than google it; the bewilderment in his baby blue eyes contrasting starkly with the resilience now in Jack's.

'Do you remember when you broke your arm and I had to act as chauffeur?' she asked. 'Do you still surf?'

Jack shook his head. 'No time.' And, as if on cue, his mobile rang. 'Jess,' he explained as he pressed decline. 'I'll phone her back.'

She looked up at him and she envied Jess his attention, his love, and everything else. She knew she shouldn't, but she did. 'Must be going,' she said with a determination she didn't feel. 'Else Dad will think I've abandoned him to another night of communal living.' With the bravest of smiles, she took the keys from him and went to open her car door. All the time she was willing him to say something, even if it was only goodbye.

'I've got the pattern books,' she added when he didn't, and the silence hung heavy between them. 'We can order the wallpaper next week when I'm back.'

Yet still he didn't speak.

'Take care,' she muttered, finally turning to get into the car. The tension tight in her throat. 'I'll…' but she never finished. She could feel the warmth of Jack's hands on her arms drawing her back up to a standing position.

'Every time you go away, I think, is this it? Is this the last time I'll see you again?'

She didn't know what to say. She thought of Tom and Jess, and everything she and Jack once had, which he'd thrown away. 'We had our chance,' she said quietly.

'I know.'

'And nothing's changed – has it?'

She could see the furrows fixed across his brow, and she knew he was fighting with the answer, to make it fit the fairy-tale ending they both wanted, but he couldn't. He was as entrenched as ever and there was nothing she could do to change it.

'Goodbye,' she said, more to herself than to him. The words trapped in her memory, as he slowly released her. And she despaired of herself, of Jack, of everything she'd built up, that she could let him do this to her again. That he still had the power to make her feel as though her life were over.

And she knew she was being ridiculous, because she still had her father. She still had Tom, and she knew she should stop being greedy and be grateful for that. But she couldn't, because, at that moment, she didn't have Jack. She didn't have the man standing beside her, holding the car door open for her. And without him in her life, nothing else seemed to matter.

Chapter 9

Robertsville stood in the middle of the Sussex Downs. A collection of cottages from every century were dotted along a high street, and the roads leading off. Aunt Beth's house was at the end of one such road. It was where Victoriana met the country, with fields and woods spilling out to the horizon beyond. It was also where Isy had spent many happy summer holidays as a child while Jack had stayed behind in Devon to help her father.

'I don't suppose you know anything about Jack's family?' she asked, once Frank was safely asleep in the conservatory.

Her aunt looked up from slotting the lunchtime plates into the dishwasher. Her years as a teacher gave nothing away. 'And why do you want to know now?' she asked, fixing her with a pair of eyes as large as Isy's.

It was a good question and Isy wasn't sure she had the answer. 'I suppose you could call it unfinished business?'

Her aunt smiled. 'Do you know, my dear, I was waiting for you to ask this six years ago.'

'So, you'll tell me now?'

'No, my dear, I'm afraid I can't.'

Isy frowned. Her aunt was almost as infuriating as her father. All the way here from the hospital, she'd tried, tactfully, to prise information from Frank. Each time, she was met with a gentle rebuff. Until finally, the satnav had frayed his patience, with its constant 'recalculating', and she'd heard him say that there were, 'Some things, my dear, that are best left unsaid. Things which really, if I'm being blunt, are none of your business.'

The only problem was that she didn't see it that way. Six years ago, things were different. Jack had deceived and deserted her, in equal measure, and both were unforgiveable. So, she didn't care about his reasons, only his actions. Now, though, it was so much more complicated than that. She felt guilt. She felt regret. But most of all she felt an unbearable sense of loss.

'Is everything OK?' Her aunt interrupted her thoughts. 'Only you seemed very preoccupied at lunch?'

'That's probably because I was. You see, Auntie, I think I might be going mad.'

'Over anything in particular?'

'Over Jack, the man I swore to hate. Only I don't hate Jack, that is. And I'm not really mad, am I, as nothing's happened? Not really. Not yet. And that's good, isn't it?' She paused to catch her breath and gauge her aunt's reaction.

'So that's why you want to know about him, is it? About his family. You want to know if you should give him a second chance, don't you?' her aunt surmised.

That wasn't quite how Isy would have phrased it, because she had absolutely no intention of hurting Tom, but she was past the point of semantics. 'I want to know why he sent me away. Is that so very wrong?'

'Then why don't you ask the man himself?'

'Because I can't. Because I know what he'll say. He'll tell me it's private, that I wouldn't understand. And he's right, of course. I don't, but I want to. I want to try and make sense of everything that's happened and try and make it right. But I can't do that if no one will talk to me, if no one will tell me what it's all about.'

Her aunt looked at her kindly, as though she was a child again. 'Come with me, my dear,' she said, passing her a cup of coffee and leading her into the sitting room. 'Let's go and sit down, shall we, and you can tell me exactly what it is that's troubling you and what you want to know.'

'Everything, Auntie. I want to know everything.'

Her aunt patted the seat on the sofa next to hers. 'That's a very tall order, my dear, but I'll tell you a little about the family, and we'll see where we go from there, shall we?'

Isy settled down next to her, against flower covered cushions, the fumes from the coffee filling the air. Her aunt took a sip from her mug, before leaning back and giving her her undivided attention.

'They were such good friends at school, your father and Jack's. He was a good-looking boy, too, was our Tony. He had his parents' Italianate looks, dark hair and skin tone, which is, of course, where Jack gets his colouring from.' She paused, her eyes filled with the sadness of time, and Isy wished she could tell her aunt to stop, that it didn't matter, but she couldn't, because it did. It mattered immensely.

'And?' she prompted as gently as she could. 'You were saying?'

'They died, my dear, his parents, both of them, just before he left school. Tony's, that is, not Jack's. Some car accident in Italy, which was such a shock, as he could have made something of himself, gone to university, but he couldn't.'

'Why ever not?'

'He had a younger brother, you see, who was always in trouble. He had to stay to look after him.'

This was news to Isy. 'So, Jack has an uncle?'

Her aunt shook her head. 'Not now. He died in his twenties, in prison.'

'And his mother – Jack's mother?'

Her aunt faltered. The smile that was never far away vanished. 'I never met her,' she said finally.

'Never?'

Beth shook her head, her hair, a mass of white, fixed in a bob that had been that way as long as Isy could remember. 'I'd left the area, you see, gone to teaching training before he met her.'

'But you must have heard about her? Dad must have spoken about her? If she was alive when Jack left, Dad must have met her on several occasions. He must have said something?'

If he had, her aunt wasn't telling. She'd come to the end of her story. If there was more to tell, then it was for someone else; for Jack, her father but not for her, and Isy respected her for it, but she couldn't let it go.

'What about Jack's father?' she persisted. 'I know he's dead because he has to be. Else Jack would have mentioned him when he told me he had a mother. What happened to his father?'

'Why do you really want to know all of this, my dear? What good will it do you now, going back in time? You gave up on the man when he hurt you so badly. And don't get me wrong, I don't blame you. You have every right to be happy and follow your dream. To be your own person, just as your mother did before you. She'd have been so proud of you.'

Isy felt tears prick her eyes. 'Would she? Would she really approve of me for having turned my back on someone who needed my help?'

'I don't think Jack needs your help, my dear. I understand he's very happy down in Devon with Jess and the business. And you've got your life in London, with Tom. Leave the past alone, my dear, and concentrate on your future, on what's important to you, because once you know that, everything else will fall into place.'

Later that evening, Isy found herself doing just that, her mind abuzz with more questions than answers as she pulled up outside Tom's flat. The pinnacle of twenty-first century design, with its lifts, and concierges, and heating that actually worked.

And she knew she should be happy living in Battersea, in a world where even the blinds could be closed at the click of a button, but she was no longer so sure. She needed Tom to be here to complete the picture, but he wasn't even answering his phone.

Working late, was the last text she'd received. *Might be an all-nighter XX.*

So, she gave up trying and poured herself a large glass of wine instead, before wandering over to the balcony. London lay before her, lit up like a gigantic sparkler, with bursts of electricity shimmering their way along the Thames.

It was a view to admire. A statement of success, that came at a price, and she knew Tom had paid heavily for his. It was his way of proving himself to his father, one of London's leading barristers, and she admired him for it. How could she do anything else? The commitment. The drive. Only she wasn't sure if it was enough for her. Not anymore. Loneliness was niggling away at her when it never had before, and she was on the point of giving up trying to analyse her thoughts, when her mobile went.

'Tom?' she asked, grabbing the phone without looking.

'No, Jack.'

'Oh.'

'Don't sound so disappointed and don't hang up on me.'

'I'm not, on either charge.'

'That makes a novel change.'

She could almost hear the note of thanks in his voice. 'Can we FaceTime?' she asked, trying not to sound as excited as she felt.

'You can try.'

She hung up, clicked the icon, redialled, and waited for him to appear. Her image shot to the corner of the screen. 'It might not work very well,' came his voice as his face joined hers. 'Bad reception.'

'Where are you?' Her eyes scanned the background, to try to separate him from the night.

'I've been with Jess, at her cottage. We've just finished work.'

She glanced at her watch. It was almost ten. 'Are you alone?'

'Are you?'

She thought about it for a moment, as a multitude of lies shot through her but she couldn't be bothered. 'Yes,' she said as his face showed his displeasure in miniature. 'But it's all right because he's working late, like you.'

'Are you sure?'

It was on the tip of her tongue to ask him exactly what he meant, when she realised she was straying into conversations she'd rather not have. 'I think I should go.'

'Don't. Please.' The urgency in his request took her completely by surprise. 'There's something I need to tell you...'

She stared at the man at the other end of the phone. She could almost feel his determination and she was scared. Was this the moment she'd been dreading since her return, when he was going to tell her about his love for Jess? The new woman in his life?

'I can't do this,' she declared, 'not now.' And before he could say another word, she hung up on him. When he phoned back, she didn't answer. When Tom finally phoned, she didn't answer. Instead she took her dinner for one out onto the balcony where she sat and watched as the world partied from afar, while the lights slowly faded on yet another day.

Jack cursed silently as he went back inside Jess's cottage and sank down onto the sofa, his mind going over and over what he'd wanted to say and what he actually had. 'You've got to be the most bloody infuriating woman alive,' he blurted out in sheer exasperation.

'And yet you still love her.' Jess was standing at the bottom of the stairs, wrapping her dressing gown around her slender frame.

'And yet I still love her.'

She smiled, the gentlest of smiles, and he wished it wasn't so. That he could change his allegiance and spend the rest of his life with a woman who would accept him for what he was, rather than someone who chewed up his insides like a Rottweiler on heat. But he couldn't. He was a lost cause. He had been since the day he was born.

'I'm sorry,' he said, pulling himself up and onto his feet.

'Don't be, I always knew you were never mine.'

'I'm not anyone's.'

'But you want to be.'

'Once maybe.'

Jess gave him a quizzical stare which told him what he already knew. That he was deceiving no one, and he really should be going. 'Until tomorrow then?'

'We have a meeting at eleven,' she reminded him. 'Harry wants to show us the concepts. And no, I'm not going without you. Not this time. But I will, if he asks me out again, for a drink, accept his offer – what do you think?'

'I think you should go,' he acknowledged ruefully. 'He's been looking at you all smitten like since we started this project.'

She smiled. 'I'm glad we're partners.'

He gave her an affectionate kiss on the cheek. 'So am I.' And without another thought, or backward glance, he turned and left, his mind two hundred miles away with the woman whose image he could still see on his phone. An image of hope and despair, but most of all, one of sheer bloody vexation.

*

Isy was coming to the conclusion there weren't enough hours in the day. She was woefully unprepared for her meeting this afternoon, and she'd not heard from Jack since Wednesday evening. It was now Friday.

'Are you really coming down with me tonight?' she asked Tom at breakfast.

'Next week, Bella,' he said, grappling with a piece of burnt toast and his jacket. 'I said next weekend.'

She wasn't sure he had, but she didn't push it. 'So, I won't see you until then?'

'You'll see me tonight if you stay. You'll see me for the whole of the weekend if you stay.'

'But I can't, you know I can't.'

'Won't more like,' he said, but he didn't seem perturbed. It was as though he was back at boarding school, and he knew there was no good protesting. His parents would be back when they were back, which wasn't necessarily when he wanted them to be.

'You take care of yourself, Bella,' he said, standing in the doorway, with his computer case over his shoulder.

It was all so formal. He could have been a stranger rather than the guy she'd slept with last night. So, with a rush of energy she didn't know she possessed, she flew at him and gave him the biggest embrace she could manage, trying not to crush his suit. 'See, no damage,' she beamed, once she'd released him. 'Now you can go to work with a smile on your face.'

It was only when he'd left, that she realised he wasn't smiling, that he never really had. He'd watched her with a vacancy she'd not seen before, as though she'd already vanished from his life, and it didn't make for comfortable viewing.

'Do you know, you're the only man who's talking to me?' she told her father once she'd joined the A303. 'If you don't count my clients?' *And you probably won't be shortly, if you knew what I was trying to do.*

She'd started her search for Jack's father. Despite what her aunt had said, she couldn't let it go. Not now she had a name: Tony Mancini. Probably short for Anthony – Jack's middle name? And she knew he'd grown up near to where her father had lived in Woolwich, as they'd attended the same school. Friends for life, or so her aunt had hinted. So, she'd decided to start her search for a death certificate there, trawling through the internet for any site that could help. It was a laborious job and one she kept having to halt so she could concentrate on her career, not to mention what she was supposed to be doing for the Hall.

'I've chosen some patterns,' she told her father, 'for the dining room and several of the bedrooms. What happens if Jack doesn't agree?'

'Are they in budget?'

She wanted to lie and say yes, but she couldn't. 'I'm hoping he can stretch it.'

Her father's silence at the other end of the phone didn't give her a lot of hope, but she wouldn't be deterred. The sooner they finished the work, the sooner everything would slot neatly back into place. Her father would be well. The Hall would be in profit, and Jack could marry Jess. Leaving her free to return to London and spend the rest of her days trying to make it work with Tom.

It all sounded so simple when she listed it like that. Only it wasn't. Her emotions were in such turmoil that she couldn't sleep let alone think, and she needed somehow to sort herself out. But first, as she pulled into the drive, she had yet another apology to make. This time, for hanging up on the man who was coming down the steps to greet her.

'These were left for you.' Jack knew that sounded a little ungracious, but he didn't want her to think they'd come from him. 'A gift from Wiktor and Jakub,' he added, 'to thank you, I think, for your attempts at friendship.'

Isy looked across at the bunch of chrysanthemums he'd placed in a chipped vase, for safekeeping. 'How sweet,' she said, doing a frantic bit of rearranging. 'And I'm sorry I wasn't here when they left. I'm really going to miss them.'

So was Jack, but not for the same reasons, he guessed, as Isy. 'We need to talk,' he said, before he lost his nerve. *I need to tell you about Jess.*

'Do we?' She glanced up at him as though it was the last thing she wanted to do. 'Do we really? Can't it wait until the morning?'

No, no, it can't, he wanted to say, but suddenly he wasn't so sure. She was studying him with a mixture of fear and something else he couldn't quite place. It was a lethal combination and it totally scuppered his thought processes. 'Do I frighten you?' he heard himself ask.

'No, no, of course not,' she retaliated. 'Whatever gave you that idea?'

'The way you're looking at me.' *The way someone else looked at me once before?* And he could feel his heart start to race, but it wasn't with joy. This was not how he'd planned the evening, not why he'd waited up, to have her throw him to the wolves.

And before he knew what he was doing, he'd thrown his crib sheet out of the window, and was standing right in front of her, his eyes taking in everything about her, from the way she'd styled her hair, to the hint of indignation creeping across her lips.

'Jack,' she began. But he couldn't turn around and walk away. Not now. Those perfect glints of green were gazing up at him, questioning his presence a little less with every second that passed, until he knew what he had to do. He had to wipe away any doubt and show her how he felt, he had to kiss her. A gentle caress at first – he was scared to do more – while he waited for her to react and tell him where to go, to hell and beyond.

Only she didn't. He could feel her tongue begin to respond, to tease his as only Isy's ever could. An act so perfect, so indescribably sexy, that he didn't want it to end. His body pressed hard against hers, his hands slipping down her shoulders as every muscle drew her towards him. His need rising before he could batten it down, causing her to struggle, to try to push him away.

'That was wrong,' she gasped, as soon as he released her. 'So wrong, on so many levels.'

But it was good too, wasn't it? he wanted to ask. He wanted her to give voice to everything he was thinking and tell him just how much she'd missed him. That Tom was useless, that the only person she'd ever wanted was him, Jack Anthony Mancini.

Only she wasn't. She was looking at him as though he was the last person in the world she wanted, her eyes awash with guilt. 'Tom,' she managed to get out finally. 'What have we done? And Jess. It would break her heart, if she knew…' She paused. 'If she knew how you still felt about me.'

'She knows already.'

'She does?' Anxiety flooded through her face. 'And…and how does she feel about it?'

'We're business partners, Isy, nothing else.'

'That's not what her Facebook page implies.'

Then you shouldn't read it, he wanted to say. He wanted to tell her to trust him, and only him. To stop looking at him as though they'd committed a sin, because they hadn't, not as far as he was concerned, but he could tell Isy wasn't convinced, that she was thinking of Tom.

'I'm going to bed,' she said, trying to brave his gaze.

And he knew he should say something, do something, anything, to make her stay, but he couldn't. Not now. Not tonight.

'You're forgetting I'm already in love,' she muttered, as she backed away, 'with someone else.' As if the decision was really that simple. Only he knew it wasn't. That decisions seldom were, and that one day soon they'd have to choose. Truth or lies? Heaven or hell? And they'd both have to live with that decision for the rest of their lives.

Chapter 10

Isy glanced down at the name on the screen. 'I've found you,' she said sadly, almost wishing she hadn't. 'The father of the man I mustn't love.' It had taken nearly another week of furtive searching from her bedroom to track down Jack's father's death certificate. And now she finally had the details within her grasp. All she had to do was order it from the General Register Office. Yet something held her back.

'Do you fancy a meal out?' Jack had asked a few hours earlier, from the top of a ladder. 'I think we deserve a night off.'

She didn't disagree. Only she wasn't sure if she should spend it with him. Not after the kiss, or lack of an apology. Or anything really to take her mind off what had happened.

'This is not a date,' she warned him once he'd joined her on the level. 'Tom is coming down tomorrow night for the weekend, and I don't want there to be any misunderstanding between us.'

He threw her a look of casual amusement. 'I think we understand each other perfectly, don't you?'

Several hours later she still wasn't sure. She was playing a dangerous game of cat and mouse with her heart, and she didn't want to lose. Only she still wasn't aware of the rules, let alone who was Jerry.

'I'm glad to see you've removed the sign,' Jack said, without waiting for an invitation to come in.

'It wasn't doing any good anyway,' she replied, quickly pulling the lid down on her laptop, before turning around to face him. 'You're actually ready?' His appearance, momentarily, took her by surprise. Gone were the work clothes of earlier, splattered with a lifetime of stains, and in their place were a pair of hip-hugging jeans and a white shirt, which was spotless.

'You look…good,' she said, wishing with all her heart he didn't.

'So do you.' His eyes narrowed appreciatively. 'But I'm not sure how you're going to cope on the bike in that.'

She glanced down at what she was wearing. She'd slipped on a jersey dress, which clung to her curves. Perfect for driving in the confines of a car; not so great for what he was proposing. 'Why do we have to go on the bike?'

'Easier to park. The King's Head has become very popular since you left – they've got several rosettes.'

She hesitated. The last thing she wanted was to share a bike with him. It was too soon, too close, and definitely too dangerous. Only she was hungry too and fed up with heating that didn't work. So, throwing self-preservation out of the window, once again, she located a pair of old biker trousers from the back of her wardrobe. 'Promise me one thing?' she said slipping them on under her dress.

He raised an eyebrow at her quizzically.

'That you won't go too fast? That when I tug at you to slow down, you will.'

'I promise.'

She wasn't sure whether she believed him or not. All she knew was that sharing a motorbike with him, after the beauty of that kiss, was probably akin to asking Genghis Khan for a ride on his pony. And, as he passed her a helmet, she wished she'd not spent quite so long trying to style her hair. The end result was not going to look good.

Jack knew exactly what he was doing when he'd suggested the bike. It was his way of trying to rekindle their past. He was just surprised, and relieved, she'd agreed so easily.

'Wait while I lower the foot pegs for you,' he said, as she followed him outside. It was the perfect night for a trip down memory lane. Not a cloud in the sky, just a lot of muted mutterings from his fellow passenger.

'I must be mad,' she said, donning her helmet. 'Absolutely out of my mind.'

'Do you trust me?'

The helmet didn't move, and he needed her to say 'yes', to this question, at least. 'Isy?'

She appeared to give it due consideration. Then, finally, she gave him a jerky nod.

'Thank God for that. Now, could you please stop moaning and get on behind me? And, yes, you will have to touch me. I want to feel your hands on my hips, firmly on my hips, before I put it into gear.'

He could see the indignation shoot out at him from behind the helmet, and he wanted to burst out laughing. She was looking at him just as she had when he'd given her her very first lesson.

'Are you trying to kill me?' she'd asked back then. 'How will I know when to lean? And what happens if I let go of you? Or you go too fast? Or, God help us, if we have an accident – people don't see bikes – they say that all the time – and the roads are narrow around here. I could end up over the hedge, or in it, or both at the same time?'

'Do you trust me?' he'd asked her then and she'd answered yes. Yes, without hesitation. Now, it appeared, she still had some faith in him. Not quite so much, understandably, after everything that had happened, but it was a start. And, as he felt her hands position themselves securely around his hips, there was nowhere else he'd rather be.

Isy was just grateful she'd arrived at the restaurant with everything still intact. 'Wait,' she said, quickly performing a mini striptease among the cars. Jack might have decided to forgo his biker trousers in favour of jeans, but she wasn't taking any risks.

'Here,' she said, thrusting her trousers, boots, and helmet at him, before slipping on a pair of heels from out of her backpack.

'Are you sure you don't want to give me your jacket too?'

She threw him a look of mock surprise. 'It's cold,' she added, just in case he'd missed the point. 'I need all the layers I can get.'

It was only when she reached the old oak door of The King's Head that she realised it wasn't just the weather that was making her shiver.

'Are you sure this is a good idea?' she asked nervously. 'What if I see someone I know – if they blame me for everything that's happened with Dad? For not being around to help?'

'Then they'll have me to answer to.' His voice was warm and reassuring, his body even more so. And she was grateful for his presence, just as she'd been on the bike, when her hands had finally grabbed hold of his hips, as though they'd never been away.

At first glance, The King's Head was full of strangers. The beams crowded in on Isy as they always had, but gone were the multi-coloured carpets, the villagers escaping for a pint and a moan. In their place were newly laid tiles in a limestone hue and people dressed to impress.

'The conservatory's through there,' Jack said, his voice steering her from behind, past tables packed with diners, towards a modern extension of wood and glass, and the first person she actually recognised.

'Matt,' she beamed, when they reached the man holding the menus. 'I didn't know you were back – that you worked here?'

Their friend from school tried to hide his surprise but failed miserably. She could see him glance over her head at Jack, with a question mark as long as his face. *Don't ask,* she wanted to say. *It's beyond complicated.* Only she didn't have a lifetime to explain. 'So, you're back in Devon,' she remarked, to try to gain their attention. 'I thought you were still in the hub at Kings Cross?'

'Sold my app for some serious money. Decided to invest some of it down here. Got Mum and Dad involved. Something for them to do.'

Isy glanced at where Matt was indicating. She could see the portly figure of his father behind the bar.

'Makes a change from him being under it,' Matt added with an affectionate grin.

Isy smiled up at him, at the fully shaved head of the first boy she'd kissed, before he turned away and led them to their table. The room spread out before her as beams of timber rose up from the walls and spanned the space with precision planning. And beneath the canopy, with its starlit sky, sat their fellow diners, with plate after plate of appetising aromas before them.

'Got your old man to thank for the build, him and Jack,' Matt said, pulling back the chair for her. 'How's he doing?'

'Dad's doing just fine,' she said gratefully, while Jack offloaded the biking gear onto a spare seat beside him, and finally shook his surfing partner by the hand.

'Enjoy,' Matt said, handing them both menus. Only she had the distinct feeling that he wasn't just alluding to the culinary treats on offer.

'So, just how many women have you brought to this restaurant?' she asked, once they were alone.

Jack leant back in his chair and gave her a whimsical smile. 'Let me see, it's been open just under two years, so that would make…?'

And she could have flung something at him if there was only something dispensable to hand. 'Do you come here with Jess?'

'I've come here with you.'

'Not to the restaurant.'

'No, but to the pub, when you didn't want to go to the Duck

and Drake. It was the only way your father would allow you to go out in the early days.'

She found herself grimacing at the recollection.

'He just cared for you,' he reminded her. 'Don't knock it.'

She didn't. It just made her more determined than ever to find out about Jack's. 'Your father, you never talk about him?'

'And you never ask.'

'I'm asking now.'

'Well, I'm not talking about him.'

And Isy knew she should let the subject drop. That she really should choose between the beef wellington and lamb shank, but she'd never been very good at doing what she was supposed to do. 'Why is everything about your childhood a secret? I ask Dad, he tells me to mind my own business. Even Auntie Beth avoids the subject, when she can.'

'Then perhaps you should too?'

'I won't judge you, Jack, I really won't.'

He glanced across at her as though that was exactly what he thought she'd do, and she hated herself for pushing him where he didn't want to go. But then what else could she do? When she could sense there was still so much more he hadn't said?

'You kiss me as though you still love me. You want me to trust you, I know you do, but how can I do that, if you don't trust me with the truth?'

'Trust isn't always about knowing everything, Isy. It's sometimes about having faith in what you don't know. It's about having faith in me.'

There was a silent plea behind the words. She could hear it in his voice, and she wanted to agree, she really did. Only how could she when she'd been here before? Six years earlier?

'I think I should go,' she said, once Matt had taken their orders. 'As soon as the Hall's finished. I think I should go back to London.'

'Because I won't talk to you?'

'Because there's no point in staying.'

The words were softly spoken, but they had the impact of a force ten gale, and she regretted them immediately. Hitting him where it hurt wasn't going to resolve anything. Nor was running away again. She'd have to order his father's death certificate the moment she got home if she was to have any chance of helping Jack face his past.

The ride back to the Hall was a silent affair, with Isy wishing she'd handled things a little differently. She'd never set out to ruin their evening and, in fairness, Jack had done his best to get over it. Only she couldn't. It had niggled away at her, and Tom's phone call, once they were home, wasn't helping.

'Bit of a problem, Bella.'

'Challenge,' she corrected hopefully. 'Challenge.'

'Can't get down tomorrow. Bit of a last-minute hitch. The Petersons are over from the States. Need to entertain them. Don't suppose you can get up here?'

She glanced across to where Jack was sitting in the study, calculating the cost of the wallpaper she'd chosen. And it was so tempting to say 'yes' and escape from him while she still could. From the smell of lime plaster, the dust on everything, and hit the town looking like luxury, rather than some vertically challenged angel from hell.

'Will you be down on Saturday?' she asked quietly.

'I doubt it, as I'll need to be around for the weekend. You can manage without me, can't you?'

'I thought we were going to Dartmouth, to the yacht?'

'I've cancelled that too – you do understand, don't you? It's business.'

She smiled weakly. Of course, she understood. She'd always understood. That what Tom needed to do always came first. It was only recently she'd realised that it was not only that, it was what he *wanted* to do that came first too. That the two were actually synonymous and that he'd never really had time to consider her.

Jack was conscious of the silence, that the sound of Isy's laughter had vanished from his mind. It had ever since he'd refused to answer any of her questions earlier in the evening. And he wished it wasn't so. That he could find some way to reach out to her before it was too late. To try to make her see that what might seem so simple to her was a minefield for him.

'Everything OK?' he asked, joining her in the drawing room.

She was sitting on the sofa, surrounded by a multitude of swatches. 'Absolutely fine,' she said.

Only he knew it wasn't. 'Do you want to talk about it?'

She shook her head. 'I think I'll go up,' she said, pulling herself up onto her feet. 'It's been a long day.'

'Do you need anything?' he offered. 'A drink? Chocolate? A hug?' *Me?*

She appeared to consider him for a moment, those large eyes taking in every feature of his face. 'A hug. I could really do with a hug.'

Jack wondered if he'd misheard, his heart missing more than a beat. 'From anyone in particular?' he asked, trying to play it cool.

'From you, you idiot. Just so long as you promise me that's all it will be.'

Only he couldn't. He was cursing himself for not having stopped at 'chocolate'. How could he possibly promise her restraint when he was still recovering from the bike ride home? From feeling those hands upon his hips? And now she wanted more, much, much more; she wanted his whole body, every electrifying impulse of it. Yet he held out his arms to her all same.

'A moment of weakness,' she muttered, as he drew her towards him. 'Nothing else.'

Are you sure? he wanted to ask, but he didn't dare. Instead, he allowed himself to soak up every single second in case this was the last there ever was. Her body pressed tightly against his, her perfume, the soft scent of her hair stoking every emotion he had, while he struggled for control.

'Better now?' he ventured, when she showed no signs of moving.

'Much, much better,' she mumbled into his shoulder.

'Good.' Only it wasn't for him. It was no bloody good at all, because he was trapped in a nightmare he couldn't control. A masochistic twist of fate, where he had her there in his arms, but he couldn't do what he wanted to do. He couldn't sweep her off her feet and take her where he wanted to go or say the things he wanted to say.

Instead, he tried to pull away gently while he still could, before he went too far. 'Isy,' he began, trying to steady his voice. 'I think we…no, you…,' he quickly corrected himself, 'I think you should go to bed, before it's too late.' But still she clung to him, that bundle of persistence, refusing to let him go.

'Thank you,' she said, finally raising her eyes to meet his, 'for this, for being here for me, as a friend.'

He glanced down at her. That wasn't entirely how he'd define it, but he knew how she wanted it to be. So, with a gesture born of old, he traced a few stray hairs away from her forehead. 'I assume Tom's not coming down tomorrow, now?'

She gave him a brief acknowledgement. 'But it's all right because I'll be going up to London later next week. I'll see him then.'

'And that will make it all better, will it?'

'You know it has to.'

No, no he didn't. Not when she looked at him like that. 'You could stay,' he said, before he could stop himself. 'You could stay here with me.'

And he willed her to say yes, before he went mad. To wipe away the look of guilt he could see in her eyes, telling him what a bloody fool he was to think, let alone hope, she might still want a guy like him, when she could have Tom. And, suddenly, it was all he could do not to break down in front of her, there and then, and tell her everything.

Only Jack knew he wouldn't feel better at the end of it. That she wouldn't feel better at the end of it. And that whatever they had, however distant it felt at times, would be quashed under the weight of his confession. And then there'd be no way back for either of them, ever again.

*

'Sit down here, my dear, and tell me all about it. You have no idea how frustrating it is being here, in Sussex, and not knowing what's going on.'

Isy's father didn't look frustrated, though. In fact, he looked surprisingly relaxed. The lines of constant anxiety had eased into creases of resignation, as though he'd finally realised he couldn't do everything. And she was grateful for his acceptance, that she no longer had to persuade him that inactivity was not a sin.

'Jack's finished the groundwork, apart from the planting,' she said, joining him in the conservatory. 'Lime plasterers are on their second coats and we've got the wallpaper and fabric ordered. Slight tussle over the colours but I won.' She gave him a muted flash of triumph, which hid the extent of the tussle. How Jack had only capitulated after the night of the cuddle. 'Everything's going according to plan,' she added with so much confidence she almost believed it herself. 'Even the conservation officer is pleased with us!'

'And you, my dear, how are you coping with it all?'

That was a little trickier to answer. She'd had a heart to heart with Tom when she'd arrived back in London that week. Only she wasn't sure she'd actually achieved anything.

'Do you think we can talk?' she'd asked when he'd finally come home on her first evening back. 'Only I know you're out tomorrow and I go back on Friday?'

He was looking through the freezer while she was talking, and she knew he was hungry, but she'd waited over a week to say these things and she couldn't wait any longer.

'I need you to tell me if we have a future,' she said, before he could catch his breath. 'I need you to tell me why it looks as though someone's been sleeping on my pillow.'

'That's easy,' Tom replied, without hesitation. 'I've been using both of them. Next,' he asked, finally retrieving a pizza for one from the freezer.

'Us,' she began, feeling her stomach tie itself up in knots. 'Is there a future for us?'

'Surely that's not for me to answer, Bella. You're the one who's decided to move to Devon, without consulting me. Then tell me you're staying there for three months. Surely, you're the one who should be answering the question about whether we have a future, not me?'

It was the clear logic she'd come to expect of Tom, to love. Only she wasn't the client here, she was his partner. Surely, she deserved more? 'Do you want to be with me?'

'Of course, I do, but you're hardly ever here, Bella.'

'But I will be, in less than three months. I'll be here forever, if you want me to be?'

He didn't reply. He continued slipping his pizza out onto a baking tray, back in his own world, where she didn't exist. For two wonderful years, she'd been allowed to share his space, and believe she meant something to him. Tonight, though, for the very first time, she was no longer so sure. That it wasn't just distance that drove you apart, it was the ability to adapt, to work out what was important and to cling to it, with all your strength, before it slipped away from you for ever.

'Yes, Dad,' she said, flicking her mind back to the present.

'Everything's just fine. Tom doesn't care for me as I've left him alone in London, and I think, no, I know Jack still loves me, but he won't leave Devon. Personally, I'm thinking of doing a runner and emigrating to Australia or becoming a nun. What do *you* think I should do?'

Her father had given his opinion. He'd told her about her mother, the beautiful artist he'd met on the steps of the National Gallery. How he'd chased after her scarf as the wind had tossed it higher and higher, almost out of reach. That Isy should seize love wherever she found it, only she was far more interested in the one thing she hadn't told him. How she'd picked up the envelope containing Jack's father's death certificate from her address in Battersea.

She'd not opened it there. It didn't feel right in Tom's flat or in her aunt's home. But now she was back in Devon, there was nothing holding her back. Jack was out. She was by herself, in her bedroom. So, retrieving the envelope from her case, she placed it on the dressing table, her conscience playing with all the permutations, until she decided there was only one thing for it. Running her finger under the seal, she tore it open, and pulled out the contents.

She was hoping for an address, an indication of the next of kin, anything that would be of use in her search for his parents. She glanced at the piece of paper. 58 Osdine Road. Maria Mancini. Cause of death? She quickly scanned the typing. Haemorrhage due to multiple stab wounds to chest.

She looked at the name of the deceased. Antonio Nicolo Mancini. There was no mistake. She glanced at the date of death.

The area in which he lived. His profession. Surely, there was some error here? Murder? Manslaughter? This sort of thing happened on the TV, or in books. To other people, not to people she knew. Or people she loved.

She put the certificate down on the bed, then picked it up again, as though by doing so, the words would rearrange themselves into something she could understand or accept. And when they didn't, she was faced with the consequences of what she'd done.

Jack's father hadn't died from an act of nature. It was an act of man. And there was someone out there with blood on their hands, who'd killed the father of a boy aged five. The only questions were who and why? And, most importantly, did Jack know? Did he have any idea as to how his father had met his death?

Chapter 11

Hydrangeas or rhododendrons – or should he order both? White or blue? Pink or red? Or a mixture of the two? God, what was happening to him? He used to be decisive. He used to score tries. Win surfing competitions. Have women offer him things to make a gigolo cringe.

Now he couldn't even make a simple choice about planting.

'Do you want to go away and think about it?' the lady at the nursery asked, a weather-beaten woman with a sympathetic smile.

'No,' he said more curtly than he'd intended. 'I don't have time.' And that was the problem. He didn't have time to do anything properly anymore. He was so thinly spread that he was surprised he'd not evaporated into the ether all together.

Isy, he thought, as he felt his mobile vibrate in his pocket. She was phoning to tell him she was leaving Robertsville. The anticipation providing the adrenalin shot he needed.

Only it wasn't her, it was Frank. 'Don't suppose she's with you?' he asked as Jack threw an apologetic glance to the woman in front of him. 'Only she's not answering her phone.'

'Isn't she with you?'

'Left here hours ago. I know she's back at the Hall as she sent me a text. Just wanted to let her know she left a folder behind. I'll courier it to her tomorrow. Can you tell her?'

With abject apologies to the queue behind, Jack slipped his mobile back in his pocket. 'I'll be back tomorrow morning,' he promised the lady at the counter, 'with a decision and the biggest order you've ever had!'

Now, though, he had an errand to run and another lady to see. Someone who'd not contacted him when she should, which meant one thing and one thing only. She was up to something. He could sense it like a rain cloud on a hot summer's day. All he needed to do was find out what. And he could do that much better once he'd had a shower and grabbed a clean set of clothes.

Isy hadn't been in Jack's room since that night at the cove, her memory wrapping it up in mothballs and parking it so far out of reach that she'd only glimpsed it fleetingly in her dreams. Now, though, as she stood on the threshold, it spread out before her in glorious technicolour. Everything just as she remembered it to be. A man's room with few mementoes, just a multitude of memories, from the bed he'd rescued from a skip and then restored, to the graduation photo she'd given him from Sheffield. And, there, on his chest of drawers, was the raffia bowl she'd made him in junior school.

'For your jewellery,' she'd said with a pride it didn't really deserve.

He never wore jewellery, but he'd kept the bowl for his loose change. She smiled, touched that he still did. Now all she needed to do was find out if there was anything else he was keeping, within these walls, that might help her discover the truth about his past.

Opening the doors to his wardrobe, she peeped inside. His clothes stared back at her; a slightly untidy pile of jeans, jumpers, and tops shoved between the shirts. 'I shouldn't be here,' she muttered under her breath, the guilt eating away at her, as she looked at the garments he wore. 'And I wouldn't be here if only you'd talk to me. If only you'd realise all I want to do is help.'

Only her plea for understanding was cut short. She could hear the front door being opened and closed. Then the stairs begin to creak. Trying hard not to panic, she shut the wardrobe doors as quietly as she could and was about to creep out of his room when she realised there wasn't time. His footsteps were getting closer and closer. So, she had to do the unthinkable. She had to squeeze herself under his bed, where no self-respecting mouse would go, and try not to inhale a generation's worth of dust.

Seconds later, she could hear his door open, and footsteps coming towards her. Something heavy was thrown onto the bed, probably his jacket. Then, she guessed, a belt was being undone as a pair of jeans came jangling to a crash on the floor beside her, covering his boots.

You're meant to take them off downstairs, she wanted to say, *the boots not the jeans. Those you're meant to keep on.*

As though he'd read her mind, she could see the action being carried out in reverse. The jeans were definitely being pulled back on.

'Isy, I know you're here. I can smell your perfume.'

She could see the boots move away, with more purpose than style. Hear the wardrobe door being opened and shut. And then they returned.

'You do realise that no one's swept under there since Mrs White left five years ago, don't you? And I'm not even sure she did.'

Tell me about it, she wanted to say, trying desperately not to sneeze.

'And that you will eventually have to come out?'

Not until you're gone.

'Alternatively, I could just bend over and drag you out…'

'Don't you dare.' Damn, she'd said that out loud. She heard him burst out laughing. Quickly whipping her hand to her ear, she removed a silver hoop. 'Found you,' she declared with a flash of divine inspiration, as she scrambled head first into full view, her clothes covered in more dust than a vacuum cleaner bag. 'You were saying?'

'I was wondering what you're doing in my room? If you wanted a tour of the highlights, you only had to ask?'

'I was looking for you.'

'What – under my bed?'

'I lost an earring,' she retorted, restoring the piece of silver to her ear. 'And, by the way, you really do need to vacuum under there,' she added with a couple of well-timed sneezes. 'Enough dust to start an allergy.'

'I'll remember that for the next time you decide to lose an earring.' He handed her a box of tissues from the top of his chest of drawers.

'Thanks,' she said pulling out a few. 'So glad you retrieved your jeans, else this could have been so much more awkward.'

And with a smile of pure innocence, she aimed for the door. Helping him to face his past was proving to be a little more stressful than she'd first envisaged, but now she at least knew where he kept his secret documents. In a small black box marked *Private*, stored with the dust and a very sturdy padlock under his bed.

I need some metal cutters.

'And why, Miss Forrester, did you need to purchase said item?'

'Because, your honour, I wanted to prise open a box that isn't mine and look at things that don't belong to me.'

Isy could hear it now, and she was the first to admit her idea had some serious flaws. It wasn't the worst plan she'd ever concocted, but it certainly wasn't one of her better ones either. It was only when she'd joined Jack in the kitchen, she realised she couldn't do it. She couldn't betray his trust.

'I thought we could have a Chinese?' he said, passing her the menu. 'I'll phone the order through and then go and collect. Unless you want something else?'

She shook her head. 'I'll have what I always have,' she said, shelving her thoughts for the moment.

'And what will that be – it's been a while?'

Grabbing a pen from one of the drawers in the kitchen, she ticked her order. 'This is a very well used menu,' she remarked, passing it back to him with its plethora of ticks from the past.

'Your father and Jess,' he offered before she could ask.

'How is Jess?' she asked, hating herself for feeling jealous of her oldest friend.

'Hoping to see you this weekend.'

'I've not forgotten. I thought I'd pop in and see her after Mrs White's visit here tomorrow. We're going to discuss menus, as I need to book the caterers next week.'

He gave her a smile of approval. 'Glad to see you've got it all under control.'

'Oh, but I do. I have everything under perfect control.' She looked back up at him, at the inquisition in those eyes. *Everything,* she thought sadly, *except what to do about you.*

Chapter 12

'Would you like cupcakes, Mrs White, as well as a proper cake? They're all the rage these days. You can get such fancy toppings – all colours. We could get them done in gold – for your golden anniversary?'

Mrs White was sitting in the kitchen at the Hall. 'Do you know, Miss Isabella, I don't think anything's changed since I was here last. How are you all going to manage with your father being so poorly?'

'We're going to do just fine, don't you worry about it. It's amazing what you can get done on a few hours' sleep.'

Actually, that wasn't entirely true. She'd almost missed a vital clause in one of her agreements last week. She was having to check everything more than once, to make sure she was concentrating, and she was dreading having a board meeting with one of their major clients, as she wasn't entirely sure that Millie and she were working in total harmony. But then nothing ever did go according to plan. Not in the real world.

'Master Jack, has he fully recovered?'

'From what?'

'From sorting out Miss Jess's boyfriend, that's what. A mean brute of a man.'

She wondered if she'd just flicked over to the wrong show on the remote and needed to flick back. 'He appears to be doing fine, now,' she said cautiously, 'as well as can be expected. You're right, though, it was a shock, a terrible shock.'

'Always knew that Mickey Lancing was a wrong 'un. Led 'is poor mother a right song and dance, 'e did, while 'e was at school. Then, when 'e was 'ad up for thieving, right near broke 'er 'eart. Why Miss Jess said yes, that she'd walk out with 'im, Gawd only knows.'

Isy loved Mrs White's use of the vernacular, but she wasn't so sure about the content. Mickey Lancing? Mickey Lancing with tattoos and muscles the size of footballs? Who lived in the next village and was banned from every pub this side of the Tamar? What the hell was Jess getting involved with someone like that for, when she could have had anyone?

It was a question she needed to ask, as soon as Mrs White left. But first she had to go out and buy Jess the biggest bunch of flowers she could find, to apologise for being the worst best friend ever. For never being around when people needed her the most.

'How beautiful,' Jess exclaimed, staring at an abundance of roses and lilies, all tied up with strands of pale pink raffia. 'But you shouldn't have.'

'I think I probably should, from what I hear. So how about I pour us both a glass of wine and you can tell me all about it?'

'I don't have any – wine, that is. Jack drank the last.'

'Now, why doesn't that surprise me? But no problem, I've come prepared.' Isy delved into her shoulder bag and produced a bottle of Chardonnay. 'Amazing what you find in here,' she added with a smile. 'I've bought crisps and sandwiches too.'

Minutes later they were both sitting in seats, either side of the stove; plates balanced carefully on their laps, as the years flew away from them, along with the wine.

'He said he'd reformed,' Jess began, offering her another glass. 'Mickey, that is. That he wanted to go straight. So, I gave him a job at the factory, in charge of security. I know, I know, looking back, I was so naïve, but he was good, initially, really good, and I thought I was doing the decent thing, rehabilitation and all that, and then...'

Isy studied her friend with a mixture of admiration and disbelief. 'And then?'

'And then he asked me out and wouldn't take no for an answer.'

'So, what did you do?'

'I went out with him – what else could I do? I was scared, Isy, really scared of what he might do if I said no.'

'And...and where exactly does Jack fit into all of this? Mrs White went very quiet when it was clear that I hadn't got a clue what she was talking about. And I'm fed up with everyone giving me the silent treatment. I couldn't be less informed about anything if I tried.'

Jess leant forward in her chair and fixed her with a pair of unusually anxious blue eyes. 'Hasn't Jack told you?'

'Jack tells me nothing. No, that's not true. He tells me he's not going out with you, is that true?'

Jess nodded. 'He's not going out with me.'

'Then why did you put a post on Facebook saying differently?'

'Because…'

'Because?'

'Because he's protecting me,' Jess said, looking shamefaced. 'I never meant to upset you. I didn't think you cared any longer, what happened to him, who he went out with. If I had, I'd never have let him do it.'

'I didn't…don't…' Isy gave a wave of dismissal. No point introducing even more confusion into what was turning out to be a very confusing weekend. 'Mrs White said that something had happened, and I don't think she was referring to his role on social media?'

Isy could see Jess was toying with her loyalties. Whether to betray the man who'd protected her or the friendship of the woman he loved. 'I did ask him to tell you,' she said quietly, 'but I suspect he thought he was saving me if he didn't, if you didn't know what a fool I've been.'

'You've not been a fool,' Isy said instinctively. 'There's nothing stupid about being afraid.'

'But you've never been afraid of anything in your entire life.'

'That's not true, I was terrified when I first went up to London.'

'But you stayed there. You didn't come back.'

'And *you* gave that Mickey guy a chance. I don't think I'd have done that, which makes you better than me.'

Jess smiled up at her with so much appreciation it made her want to cry. 'Now,' she said gently, 'please tell me, in your own time, about Jack's role in all this, because from what Mrs White implied, I have a feeling that it was more than offering his services as a surrogate boyfriend.'

*

Jack was lying on his back on an improvised scaffolding rig, painting the intricacies of flora and fauna around the centrepiece of the drawing-room ceiling, when Isy returned home. She stared up at him, at his paint splattered overalls.

'Could you come down here a moment?' she asked as calmly as she could.

'Not really, Isy, I need to finish this before I lose the light. Can't it wait?'

'No, not really.'

'If it's about Mrs White and the menus, you can tell me while I paint. Contrary to popular belief, men *can* do two things at once.'

'It's about Jess.'

'Jess?'

'Yes, I saw her today. So, I'd be grateful if you could get your arse off that platform and down here. I'll be in the kitchen when you do.'

It didn't take him long to decide what his priorities were. He could tell by her tone she didn't want to discuss cupcakes. Putting the paintbrush into a can of water, he wiped his hands on a piece of rag. Sure enough, his mobile was showing several messages, all of which were from Jess.

She knows, sorry,' was the shortest.

By the time he'd reached the kitchen, Isy had poured them both large cups of coffee, and was sitting at the table waiting for him.

'Take your overalls off,' she instructed.

He raised a quizzical eyebrow. He had an uncomfortable feeling he knew where this was going, but since he had no wish to leave paint on the old oak chairs, he did as she'd requested. He stepped out of his overalls to reveal what he was wearing, a pair of jeans and a long-sleeved shirt.

'Do you know, it never occurred to me until today, that I've not seen you in a T-shirt since I've been back? I never thought anything of it. After all, this house is freezing most of the time, and I'm always wrapped up in several layers. But you, you never used to feel the cold.' She stood up and came towards him. 'Take your shirt off.'

'Isy...'

'Because if you don't, I will.'

'This isn't necessary,' he said, wishing she'd move away. 'This really isn't necessary.'

'Oh, but I think it is.' She raised her eyes to meet his. 'You see, I've just had a fascinating chat with Jess.' She paused, as if to gauge his reaction. 'Why didn't you tell me what was happening?'

'I tried to, several times.' And he had. 'But you wouldn't listen.'

'That's not fair. You told me you were just business partners. You never told me about Mickey Lancing.'

Jack had to concede she had a point. 'It's not as simple as that,' he said, wishing it was.

'Isn't it?' She looked up at him, confused. 'Oh, I know I should be congratulating you for doing a wonderful thing, but how can I do that when you don't tell me? When I have to find out from Mrs White? And from Jess, herself? Didn't it occur to you how I'd feel? To find out that, once again, you'd shut me out?'

'You're being overdramatic.'

'Am I? After everything you did to me six years ago, I don't think so. And I'm so fed up with feeling manipulated.'

'I've never manipulated you in my life!'

'Oh, but you have. And I fall for it, every single time. I think you need me when you don't. That I can help when you've got everyone else to keep your secrets for you. When you've never needed me, just me, for anything!'

'I've never needed anyone else,' Jack declared, astonished she could think that. 'And if you weren't going out with that bastard in London, I'd show you how much. Upstairs or anywhere else you wanted to go, I'd…'

'Fuck me, because that's all it is to you, isn't it?'

Jack felt a shiver of ice go down his spine. 'It's never been just that to me,' he said, the words catching in his throat. 'As well you know. I love you, Isy.'

'So, you once told me.' Her lips twisted into a smile, but there was no warmth in it. 'Here,' she said, passing him the sugar. 'I'm going to go and do some work. I'll stay tomorrow, then I'm going back to London on Monday.'

And for one moment, Jack wondered if this was it. If this was, finally, the end of everything? His gut clenched for the body blow to come. 'How long?' he forced himself to ask. 'How long will you be away?'

'In London? I don't know. I really don't know.'

Isy didn't look back until she reached her room. Her eyes were full of tears and she refused to shed any of them until she was alone. Did he really have no idea how she'd feel to find out, once again, he'd left her out? That he still didn't trust her with the truth?

'Don't be hard on him,' Jess had begged. 'He thought he was doing the right thing, that he was protecting me.'

'From me?'

Jess had viewed her awkwardly. 'You can be so judgemental, Isy. I know you don't mean to, but you have such high principles and it's hard, sometimes, to live up to them.'

Isy didn't know what her friend meant. She'd never judged anyone in her life, apart from Jack, and he seemed to deserve it, every single time.

'We never set out to deceive you,' Jess stressed. 'At first, I kept the bruises hidden and then, last summer, it was hot, and I'd taken my cardigan off...' She flinched at the memory. 'And Jack saw them. I tried to say I'd fallen, that I'd had an accident in the garden, but he didn't believe me. He said he'd seen bruises like that before, that he knew what it meant. So, I told him. It all sort of came tumbling out, the months and months of trying to pretend that it wasn't so, that I could handle it, that it would stop...well, it didn't.'

'What did Jack do?'

'He told me to leave him, and I tried, Isy, I really tried, but Mickey kept promising he loved me, that he'd never do it again... and...' The tears began to flow down Jess's cheeks, 'I believed him. I was such a fool.'

Isy slipped her plate onto the coffee table, next to her wine, and went over to where Jess was sitting. 'You just wanted to believe the best,' she said, putting her arm around her. 'There's nothing wrong in that.'

'I just wanted it to stop. And so, one night after he'd pushed me into the edge of a door, I managed to get myself back from his place to the factory, where Jack was still working. He took one look at me, phoned for an ambulance and then, once they'd come, he disappeared. The next time I saw him, was when I was back at my parents' house, a week or two later. He came around and told me that Mickey would never trouble me again. That he'd arranged for me to have one of the cottages on your father's estate and that, to the outside world, he was my boyfriend.'

'And,' Isy asked, her heart pounding away in her chest, 'what… what had happened to Mickey?'

'Someone saw him a few days later in Torquay. He went for Jack with a crowbar, Mickey that is. Fortunately, Jack managed to fend him off, but not before he'd made a bloody mess of his left arm. The one he broke, you know, all those years ago, surfing.'

'And Mickey,' Isy asked again. 'What happened to him?'

'I don't know. I never asked. All I know is that he left me alone. I think he's working down Plymouth way now, someone said, but I didn't ask. I don't want to know. Jack saved me, Isy. He saved me from a fate worse than death, and that's no exaggeration. I love him for it and so should you.'

Of course, Isy loved him for it. How could she do anything else? But she also hated him for it too, for the way it made her feel. And she was tired, so tired, of trying to be strong, of trying to pretend that everything was fine, when it wasn't. So why keep trying? Why not just throw in the towel and confess that nothing was as she'd hoped it would be?

Tom appeared to have lost interest. Her father had insisted he was fine for the past six years, when he wasn't. And Jack was masquerading as Branham's answer to the Caped Crusader, for everyone it seemed, except for her.

The ties of kinship and friendship had been cut, and Isy had never felt so lonely or miserable in her entire life. All she wanted to do was crawl under her bedclothes and never come out. Instead she was being forced to respond to a knock at her door, which had to be a first.

'Yes?' she made herself say.

'Does that mean I can come in?' Jack asked, 'or am I supposed to conduct this conversation from where I am?'

'You can come in.'

'Good.' He opened the door. 'I'm going down to the Duck and Drake for a game of pool. Do you want to join me?'

'Join you?' Isy did a double take. She was threatening to go back to London, potentially for good, and he was suggesting a game of pool? She wanted to ask him what part of their earlier conversation had he not understood? That he had to be the most thick-skinned creature in the universe, to think that she could want to go out anywhere with him, let alone one of their old haunts, when she stopped.

She stopped because that wasn't true. She did want to go with him. She wanted to escape to a time when she'd have followed him anywhere.

'Now why would I want to do that?' she asked, trying not to let it show. 'Go to the pub with you?'

'Because it's better than sitting in here, sulking.'

'I'm not sulking,' she retaliated, raising her eyes to meet his. 'I'm reviewing my options.'

'Ah, so that's what they call it these days, is it?' He didn't look convinced. 'Tell you what then, why don't you give me a call when you've finished "reviewing your options", and I'll come and get you?'

'And if I don't – change my mind, that is?'

He raised a bemused eyebrow. 'I think we both know you better than that, don't we?' But, before she could respond, he'd gone, leaving the room and a lifetime of memories behind him.

Isy stared at the empty space. Then back down at her laptop and the contract she was trying to draft. At that precise moment, she didn't care if it was in her client's best interests or not. All she could do was think about Jack. Did he really think she wouldn't care? That she wouldn't feel a tiny bit jealous at his loyalty for Jess? Even if he'd done it for all the right reasons?

He was right, though, about one thing. The last thing she needed right now was to be alone. She needed company. She needed some light relief. Although whether Jack qualified as either was questionable, but she soon found herself standing outside the Duck and Drake all the same.

Unlike The Kings Head, little had changed. It had been the village pub since the 1700s and, once inside, she could see the floor was as uneven as ever. The timbers were dark and decaying and there was still an all prevailing smell of smoke, that burst forth from the open fire, whether it was lit or not.

'Jess.' She could see her friend with a guy she didn't recognise.

A man who was tall and finely built, with a mop of curls in a sun-bleached shade of blond.

'Isy, this is Harry. Harry, Isy.'

He gave her a friendly smile and a shake of the hand.

'Jack's through there,' Jess said, indicating another room through the throng of Saturday night drinkers, both young and old. 'I'm so glad you're here.'

So was Isy. She was already receiving friendly greetings from several people she recognised. There was none of the antagonism she'd feared, which surprised her even more than her own courage at coming here in the first place.

Tucking the torch she'd used on her trek through the dark into a small rucksack, she took herself and her casual attire of a pair of jeans and long cardigan off in the direction of the pool room. A game was in progress. Jack was standing with his back to her talking to Andy, the son of the couple who ran the village post office.

'So, it's true, you're back,' Andy said, as she approached.

Jack turned around. A flash of pleasure, almost relief, greeted her, as he stood before her with a pint of lager in one hand and a pool cue in the other. 'If you'd phoned, I'd have come and got you,' he said, as he handed his cue to Andy and took her to one side. 'Are you staying?' he asked, lowering his voice.

'I thought you challenged me to a game?'

'Do you think you can beat me?'

'I used to.'

'Could never work out how she did,' Andy said, coming towards them, 'but she did.'

'I think he used to let me win,' Isy said, with more affection than she'd intended. She could feel Jack's proximity with every breath she took. The inquisition in those eyes asking her the very same questions she was asking herself. 'So,' she said, wishing she knew the answers, 'which one of you guys is going to get me a drink?'

Jack watched her from across the table. It was like she'd never been away. A flashback to the old days, when she'd stood there with her friends, discussing who was going out with whom, and all Jack had wanted was for her to go out with him.

'Your go,' she said, straightening up, her red strategically placed just where she wanted it to be, blocking the path to his last yellow.

'So,' he said, positioning his glass carefully on the table behind him, and picking up the cue, 'you're going to play dirty, are you?'

'I can play any way you want me to,' she replied, throwing him a challenge he couldn't resist, 'but I will win.'

He didn't doubt it for a moment. That she'd do everything she could to beat him. But he was damned if he was going to let her have it entirely her own way. Positioning his cue exactly where he wanted it, he leant forward and hit the white. The ball bounced off the cushion and straight into the yellow, just as he'd intended, the adrenaline surging through him as he knew what would come next, as the yellow pulled up just short of the pocket.

The relief in her eyes, the twinkle of defiance was unmistakable, as she found herself suddenly back in the game. And for a moment, he was oblivious to everyone else. Jess coming in with Harry. Andy leaving to buy another round. All he could think about was the woman who was potting the red, positioning her cue for her last shot. The exquisite agony of her touch as the cue slid seamlessly through her fingers, and she did what she'd been planning to do ever since they'd started the game. She potted the black. Poetry in motion, bloody poetry in motion.

'So,' she said, coming over to where he was standing. 'Do you admit defeat?' Her hands poised on his chest, her eyes sparkling up at him in triumph.

God, I love you, he wanted to say. *I bloody love you. And if things were different, I'd show you just how much. Here. Now. Wherever.* But they weren't, so he hauled in his emotions, as he'd done so many times before, and gave her a smile instead. 'One more round,' he said, 'to toast your success, and then I'll take you home. But first, I think Andy wants to take a photo.'

As Isy left the pub, she felt slightly light-headed. 'I probably should have eaten something before coming out. Do you mind if I hold on to you?' she asked, linking her arm through Jack's good one. 'Only I'm not used to the lack of lights.'

'You did well tonight.'

'I did, didn't I... A bit like old times,' she said, squeezing the security of his jacket with an affectionate tug. 'I still think you let me win.'

'Now why would I do that?'

'Because you're a good man who cares.' Now she knew she shouldn't have had that last glass of wine. She was paying him compliments!

'I like the idea of being a good man,' he said approvingly. 'Don't often hear you call me that.'

'I know, but it's not that I don't think it, because I do. But then you do things to upset me, which hurt me, and so that makes you a bad man too.'

'So, I'm good and bad.'

'Mainly good apart from today.'

'When I was bad?'

'Because you were being good. I know, it's all so confusing.' She nestled her head against his shoulder. 'But I'm glad we're friends again.'

'Isy…' He stopped and pulled her round towards him. The lane was deserted. The turning for the Hall just a few yards away. Not a cloud in the sky apart from the force of nature which she could feel bearing down at her from Jack. 'I want us to be more than friends,' he said. 'You know that don't you?'

'You see, now you're being bad,' she replied, looking up at him in earnest. 'Because I have Tom, that man in London, and he's done nothing wrong, at least nothing that I can prove, so I have to be good, very, very good…'

'Even if you don't want to be?'

'Even if I don't want to be.'

The look he gave her broke her heart. She knew there was so much more he wanted to say. Only now wasn't the time.

'I do love you,' she said, stretching up and kissing him gently on the cheeks. 'I love you very much.'

'So, I'm forgiven – for Jess?'

'For being a hero? Do you really need to ask?'

Jack hadn't opened the box under his bed since his arrival at the Hall all those years ago. He'd had no need to be reminded of the things it contained. Now, though, he needed a new home for it. Somewhere out of Isy's reach, where she wouldn't think to look for it, should curiosity get the better of her. And he knew just the place.

'Jess – I'm not intruding, am I?' He threw a glance at Harry's jacket on the sofa. Then back at the woman standing before him in her silk negligee wrap.

'Of course not,' she said. 'You're always welcome, you know that. It's just that we didn't get to sleep that early,' she added, before blushing a perfect shade of pink. 'I didn't mean it like that. You know I didn't mean it like that!'

'I think you did,' he said, smiling, 'and I'm glad for you. Seriously. You deserve to be happy, Jess. But I'm not here to pry into your sex life, I need to ask you a favour, or rather, I need to ask Harry if I can use his safe. Should I wait?'

When he returned to the Hall, Isy was where he'd left her. Half lying, prostrate, on the floor in one of the spare bedrooms, with a sanding block in one hand and a very frustrated look on her face.

'I'd forgotten how long this takes,' she said, as she broke off from sanding over the skirting boards. 'Are you sure we can't afford a decorator for upstairs as well as downstairs?'

He finished pulling on his own overalls. 'At one stage the plan was to do all the decorating ourselves.'

'And what changed it?'

'We do our own fulfilment for all the orders. It's making a huge difference to the company's profit margins.'

'If you and Jess are doing so well, why does Dad still have to open up the Hall for weddings? Couldn't the money you make help fund things?' she asked sitting up as he started sanding the architrave around the door. 'At least in the short term, until I'm earning more?'

'He won't accept any of it. I've tried.'

'But he's accepting this, what you've been putting into the renovation – I don't understand?'

'This is a loan, Isy, that's the only reason he's accepted it. I'm giving him a loan which he is determined to pay back.'

'But that's nonsense, after everything he's done for you? I'm going to have to have words with him when I see him next.'

He thought about arguing, and telling her to go easy with her father, but he had something else to impart. Something that he knew would throw any thoughts of her father and money to the back of beyond – at least in the short term.

'There's a photo of us on Facebook. It was posted this morning. Jess thought we should know.'

He was conscious of a sanding block landing heavily on the wooden planks beside him, a scrambling of feet, and an agitated appearance at his side.

'Why,' Isy began, 'did Jess think we should know?'

'I'm not on it, Facebook that is, but she knows you are.'

'That's not answering my question,' she said as she ran out of the door to find her mobile. 'Oh, no, no, no.'

He could hear the exclamation from along the corridor.

'This isn't good.'

'What isn't?'

'You know exactly what it is, don't you? That's why you're smiling. You bastard. What the hell did Andy think he was doing? Posting it on my page? And where exactly is your other arm?'

'If you don't remember that, then I'm too much of a gentleman to tell you.'

'Jack, this isn't funny. If Tom sees this, he'll never talk to me again.' She cast him a glance of pure anguish. 'Don't you ever, ever entice me into a night out, ever again, do you hear me? Don't you ever let me drink. Don't you ever let me do anything with you, ever, ever again. This is bad, bad, bad.'

She sank down in despair onto the floor.

'You're overreacting, as always.'

'Am I? Then how am I going to explain to him that I spent the whole evening playing pool with my ex-boyfriend, rather than renovating the Hall or carrying out the office work I was supposed to be doing? I'm not down here to have fun.'

'So, it was fun, then, was it?' he hardly dared to ask.

'You know it was, but it wasn't meant to be. How do you think Tom's going to feel? He'll think I've made a fool out of him and he'd be right. And God help me if his friends get to hear about this.'

He slid down on his haunches beside her. 'Maybe it's for the best?' he asked, as casually as he could. 'Leaving everything else to one side, do you really think this guy's for you?'

'He was before Dad fell ill. I was going to spend the rest of my life with him – and now look what's gone and happened!'

*

Isy wasn't sure what she was dreading more: hearing from Tom or not hearing from Tom. When the call finally came, she was in the bath, trying to soak away the strain of spending the whole day crawling about on the floor.

'You sound strange,' he said, 'are you all right?'

'Fine,' she gasped, 'too much dust. Not good for the lungs. And you?' She waited, her heart pounding against her ribcage, as the bubbles smothered her chest. *Please tell me that you haven't seen it? That a photo of your girlfriend high fiving her ex hasn't gone viral?*

'I'm going to the States next week, Bella. I'm needed in the New York office. Did I tell you?'

She couldn't tell if she was disappointed or relieved. 'Will you be back at the weekend? If you were, it would be brilliant if you could come down here, as we could really do with some help. You have no idea how long it took me today to…'

'No. Bella, you're not listening. I shall be away for several weeks. Bit of a problem out there with one of the deals.'

'Tom?'

'Yes?'

Is there any point in us going on, she wanted to say? *Only we seem to be drifting further and further apart and I'm trying really hard not to, to save what I thought we had, only…* Only she couldn't bring herself to say any of it. It was not a conversation you could have at opposite ends of a phone call.

'Do keep in touch, won't you?' she asked, as she felt the future and everything she'd once hoped for slip a little further out of her reach.

'Of course, I will, Bella, only I'm not sure how easy it's going to be.'

Then the line went dead and she knew she should phone him back and tell him she was sorry she'd not been there when he needed her, but she didn't. And when he didn't phone her back either, when there wasn't even a text, or a hint of a farewell, she knew in her heart that it was over. It just needed one of them to say it. And that a photo of Jack and her together was really the least of her problems.

Chapter 13

It was a cold afternoon in November when Isy turned the corner into Osdine Road. Autumn, with its abundance of colour, was fading fast and the street was masked in mist. Terraced houses fell away to either side of her, Victorian architecture for the masses; and nestling somewhere among this sea of conformity was number 58.

All she had to do now was find it, her heart racing a little more with every step she took at the thought she might finally get to meet Jack's mother. And, if she wasn't there, waiting patiently for her, she'd go straight to plan B. She'd find an elderly resident who knew her, and preferably one with a hot cup of tea and a large piece of cake.

She had it all mapped out. Only it had taken her slightly longer than expected to put it into action. She'd needed a reason to stay in London at the weekend, now that she couldn't use Tom as an excuse, and last week she'd finally found one.

'Tina's getting married,' she'd told Jack a few days ago. 'We're going to choose her wedding dress.' It was almost true. Tina, her friend from college, was getting married and Isy was going to help her choose her wedding dress. Only at ten in the morning, not three in the afternoon.

'Phone me later,' she'd said, wishing she didn't have to lie. 'I should be back at the flat by seven.' But now she had other things to do. She was going back to the place of his youth, where he'd lost his father. A road he probably wouldn't even recognise today judging by the cars parked there with their aspirations of hope.

What happened to you, Tony Mancini? she wondered, glancing up at the numbers as she passed them by, *that you ended your days the way you did? Did you deserve it, or were you a victim?* She couldn't imagine her father or her aunt approving of a thug, or someone with criminal tendencies, so he must have been the victim – but why?

She was just passing number 42, with its beautifully painted door in blue, and mosaic designed path, when her mobile went.

'Your father's confused,' her aunt said. 'Just wanted me to check which day you're popping in.'

'Tomorrow, auntie, I'm coming down tomorrow.' *Only you'll never guess where I am today,* she wanted to add. *I'm standing outside number 58 Osdine Road.* A house that looked as though it had seen better days. There was no beautifully painted door here. In some places, there was very little paint at all. The frontage consisted of paving slabs. No pretty patterns or intricate designs to draw the visitor in and invite them to stay.

And suddenly she realised that she'd just done a very silly thing, not telling anyone where she was. That if something happened to her in the next few minutes, it could go undiscovered for hours, days, or for however long it took them to track her phone. Suddenly she didn't feel quite so clever. Suddenly she really wanted to talk to Jack, if only to say goodbye.

'You're the spitting image of your father,' Frank would say. It was a compliment that was kindly meant, but it caused Jack more pain than pride, because he couldn't touch the man in the mirror, or speak to him. All he could do was see him. An image imprinted on his mind from a time long ago, when he'd sat all by himself on a sofa, clutching a picture book in his hand, trying so hard not to cry. Then a door had swung open and a light switched on, bathing the room in brilliance.

'Jack, my son,' said the man stepping out of the shadows with a bar of his favourite chocolate, 'what are you doing down here, all alone?'

Jack didn't reply. He'd been told to keep quiet and stay put, else something fucking awful would happen to him. And he had. He'd done what he was told to do. He'd not moved apart from to use the pot provided.

His father took in the whole scene. Anger flashed across his face, while Jack struggled to stay where he was. When all he really wanted was to be with the man who was coming towards him.

'Here, my son,' Tony said, bending down and picking him up. 'I'm not cross with you. I'm cross with me,' he added, wrapping his arms possessively around Jack and his outgrown pyjamas. 'I should never have left you for so long, but I promise you that everything's going to be all right. I'll make sure of that. We're going to have a great life, you and me, a great life, but first I need you to tell me where your mother is?'

And Jack wanted to, he really did. As he buried his head against his father's shoulder, he would have told him everything, if only he'd known what everything was. Instead, his mind was cluttered with threats and counter threats, and he was so scared of what might happen if he got it wrong, that it took all his courage to offer him the name of the man he'd grown to hate.

'Uncle Pete,' he said, tentatively raising his head to look his father in the eye.

'Uncle Pete – are you sure?'

Jack nodded as his father tried to place him back down onto the sofa. Only he wouldn't let go, his small fingers clinging to his father's jacket.

'I'm going to go and get Mrs Roberts from number 48, to sit with you. So you have to be good for just a bit longer, do you understand?'

Jack didn't. It was the last thing he wanted to do, but he knew it was important that he tried. So, cuddling the book his father had bought him last Christmas, of Thomas and the Fat Controller, he settled back down on the sofa with his new bar of chocolate, and he waited. He waited for what he'd been promised, a great life with his father, and for a time that never came.

Chapter 14

'You're a lucky girl, aren't you?'

Isy didn't feel it. She was looking up at over fifteen stone of towering testosterone, with more muscles than King Kong.

'Am I?' she asked, trying to steer her vision away from the man's bulging body to his face. It was cragged, full of the forces of nature. It reminded her of her father's, and she would have bet her legalistic brain that he was a builder.

'Yeh,' he said, chewing a piece of gum, 'just thinking of locking up.'

'Do you live here?'

He gave her the benefit of a critical stare. 'Who wants to know?'

'Just me,' she said, in a voice which she prayed installed confidence. 'Only I'm looking for someone.' And for one worrying moment, she thought he was going to say the obvious, that she'd 'found him', but he didn't.

'Someone important, is it?'

'Yes.' *More important than you'll ever know.*

The man seemed to chew on his gum a little longer, then stepped back. 'Suppose you'd better come in then.'

*

Isy wasn't entirely sure if it was fair to blame Jack for her latest predicament, but if she ended up dead because of it, she was going to come back as one mighty pissed off ghost. And he would be the first to hear about it.

The only plus to her latest exploit was that Joe Reading didn't appear to have murder on his mind. He'd got a van outside with his name on and he'd just bought this shack for over three quarters of a million quid, not much change out of a million. He'd got grandchildren, too, fifteen of them, although she was getting a little confused as to who belonged to which child, which didn't surprise her as there appeared to be several of them too, not to mention wives.

'So,' he said, as he paused for breath, 'what do you think?'

About the wives? The grandchildren? The house? She was drowning in too much information, when all she really wanted was the answers to some questions of her own. What had happened to Jack's father? Where was his mother? And why did her father bring him to live with them in Devon?

She glanced about her, at a kitchen straight out of the 1960s. The cupboards were basic by any description, almost falling off the wall. There was no sign of modern technology apart from a space for an old stand-alone cooker and another for a washing machine. The floor was scattered with linoleum and was screaming out for a major spring clean let alone removal.

'I knew someone who used to live here,' she began slowly.

'And you thought he might still be here? Do you have a name, love, for this guy?'

'Jack Anthony Mancini. His parents were Tony and Maria?'

Joe shook his head. 'Don't know them. I bought this from some Irish guy. He'd not had it long. Land Registry, they'll be your best bet if you want to know who owned it before.'

She managed a brave smile, to try to hide her disappointment. 'May I have a quick look, please, at the other rooms?'

'Be my guest, love. Tell your friends about it. I'll do them a deal when it's done. Number's on the van.'

She thanked him and found herself wandering back along the corridor. Carpets had been removed, dust peppering the wood, as she climbed the stairs, up to the bedroom, and a bathroom without a bath. Another small flight took her to an attic room. The wallpaper was peeling off in several layers. Curiosity more than design drew her to a corner near the door frame. Picking at a layer of pink tinted roses, she prised it off carefully to see what lay below. A snippet of blues and reds peeped out at her. As she looked more carefully, she could just make out the side of a small train.

Was this your room, she wondered, *where you slept? Where you swore never to return – or is there more? Did you move from here? Is that where your mother is now?*

Frustrated she was no further forward in her quest to help Jack, she went back downstairs. She thanked Joe for his hospitality and stepped back out onto Osdine Road.

It was getting dark. The trees were merging into the sky, but Isy wasn't finished. She still had that elderly resident to find, and she needed to do it now before Jack phoned for his early evening chat.

*

Isy? Where the bloody hell are you? That's what Jack wanted to say. What he'd been struggling to suppress for the past three hours, but he knew that wouldn't win him any favours. He needed to employ a little more subtlety, even if it was testing his patience to the limit. 'I assume you do know how to use a mobile phone?' he said, trying not to let it show. Then, when there was silence, 'And that you do need to speak into it for me to hear you?'

'Very funny.'

'See, you can do it. So, tell me, how did this afternoon go?'

'My what?'

'Bridal shopping with your friend, Tina?'

'Ah, that...'

'Yes, that.'

'I might have to do some more. Bridal shopping, that is.'

'Because you didn't find anything?'

'Not exactly. Or rather we did, but we need to look at more options.'

Such as? He wanted to ask. Only he wasn't sure he was ready for her response. *Is Tom back? Is that why you're lying to me? Why I know you're not telling me the truth?*

'Jack?'

Her voice penetrated his thoughts. 'Yes?' he managed to say.

'If I ask you a question, will you promise me that you'll answer it honestly? That you won't tell me it's none of my business?'

He looked across at the sofa where she normally sat. *A question – what question?* He stared at the empty space and the cushions she'd rescued from early retirement, and he knew he was in trouble.

That it wasn't Tom he should be worried about, but something potentially far, far worse.

And he was damned if he said yes. Damned if he said no, and that either response could keep her in London forever. That this might be the last conversation he'd ever have with the woman he adored. Who lit up his life with her presence, and whom he had no intention of losing a second time.

The Thames was magic by moonlight. Distant ripples smoothed out against the dark, with just a splash of illumination. And Isy loved it, but not tonight. Tonight, she was sitting on the balcony all by herself. She was wrapped up in a coat, trying hard to keep out the cold that had lodged itself in her bones ever since she'd knocked at number 48.

'I don't buy from the door,' the woman told her. 'There's a sign there.'

'That's just as well,' she replied with an optimism she was no longer feeling, 'because I'm not selling anything.'

'So why are you here?'

'I'm looking for someone,' she began, getting ready to apologise to yet another resident for interrupting their Saturday with questions of someone they'd never known. 'I'm looking for a family called Mancini, who lived at number 58.'

'Jack Mancini?'

'Yes.' And for the first time that afternoon, she felt her heart lift as hope made a welcome return. 'Did you know him?' she asked the woman standing in the doorway who couldn't have been much older than her. 'Did you know Jack Mancini?'

'No, but my gran did.'

'And where,' Isy gasped, hardly daring to breathe, 'is your gran now?'

'She died, just a few months ago.'

'Oh, I'm so sorry.' And she was for so many reasons, most of them not entirely selfless. 'And yet you say she knew him?'

'Gran never stopped talking about him. About the little boy she'd looked after on the night his father died.'

'And...and did she say anything else about him? About what happened? Where he went?'

'Something about a fight in a pub, I think, between two brothers. Over a woman, the wife of one of them. The boy's mother, I guess.' She broke off. 'I'm sorry, I can't be more precise. Gran told many stories and we didn't always listen. Never sure which were fact and which were fiction.'

'This one is fact,' Isy assured her, 'because the pieces keep fitting together.'

'Then you'd better come in,' the young woman said. 'We've been sorting out Gran's photos and I remember seeing some of a small boy. You can have them, if you think they're of any use?'

Isy could have hugged her. She may not have found the elderly resident she'd been hoping for, with promises of tea and cake, but she'd found something just as precious. Proof she was on the right track, that the death certificate was right. Jack's father *had* died at the hands of another, his brother. And his mother, the woman whom Isy was hoping to meet, probably didn't qualify for parent of the year.

*

'We're not related, are we?' Isy asked. 'Please, Jack, tell me we're not related.'

The burst of laughter at the other end of the phone was so heartfelt that she wondered what the hell he'd thought she was going to ask.

'Of course we're not bloody related,' he said. 'Whatever made you think we were?'

Because I have this photo of you aged 6½ and me as a baby, in my father's arms... Because Dad always treats you like a son... Because I'm so confused, that nothing would surprise me anymore? 'I just wondered, that's all.'

'Then don't. Do you really think he'd have stood back and let me...let us do what we did, if we were? Bloody hell, Isy, whatever gave you that idea?'

'I don't know, it was just a thought.'

'Then stop thinking!'

'Impossible. I have another question.' She heard a deep intake of breath at the other end of the phone and a clink of glass on the table. 'When did we first meet?'

'You know the answer to that.'

'Did Dad never take me to see you before that?'

'Can't you remember?'

'Nope.'

'Then he didn't.'

She wanted to ask him to try again, to give her the answer she deserved. The one she knew to be true.

'Wait a minute...'

The tone of his voice had changed, and she hated herself for what

154

she was doing, for forcing him to remember, but she had to know.

'There was an occasion when I was with Mrs Roberts, some woman who looked after me. Your father came to see me then and brought you with him. Your mother was having a bad time with the chemo, or something like that, I think, because you came alone.'

'And you remember seeing me?'

'I remember a baby who wouldn't stop crying. Why do you ask? For Christ's sake, Isy, whatever made you ask a question like that?'

Isy wished she could tell him. She'd wished a lot of things over the past few weeks, but she knew this was one of those things she couldn't divulge. And she could cope with that, just, so long as she was safely tucked away in London and he was down in Devon. What she couldn't cope with so easily was finding his Ducati parked outside her aunt's cottage the following day.

'Why didn't you tell me you were coming?' she flung at him the moment he answered the door. 'You never come here. It's Dad, isn't it – he's worse? Why didn't you phone me?'

'Calm down,' he said, as he stood back to let her in. 'Your aunt invited me over for Sunday lunch, that's all, and I thought it was rude to refuse.'

'Rude to refuse?' she almost choked. 'Since when have you worried about refusing anyone or anything? Auntie?' she asked as her aunt popped her head around the kitchen door. 'Why didn't you tell me?'

'And ruin the nice surprise?' he cut in before her aunt could.

'Now why would we go and do a thing like that?'

Her aunt threw him a look which Isy couldn't work out, before retreating into the safety of the kitchen.

'Has it not occurred to you that it might not be a nice surprise?' Isy persisted. 'That I deserved a heads-up?' She raised her eyes to meet his. A flicker of bemusement stared back at her, tinged with curiosity.

'And there was I thinking you'd be pleased to see me?' He paused as if to gauge her reaction. 'That you might have missed me?' His voice was light, but she knew the question wasn't, and it was all she could do not to give in and tell him the truth. The whole truth and nothing but the truth, that she'd missed him like crazy.

'Why *are* you here?' she asked, as lightly as she could. 'You never come to Robertsville? Why now?'

'I had some paperwork to discuss with your father. There are forms we have to fill in for the council to start the ball rolling for a wedding venue licence.'

'You could have given them to me?'

'Or I could have come to see him for myself, to see how he's getting on? Or did that not occur to you?'

It did, but she still wasn't convinced. 'I need to see my father,' she said, braving his gaze, while he stood aside to let her pass. With a quick hello to Frank, who seemed blissfully unaware of what was happening only a few yards away, she soon found herself back in the kitchen with her aunt.

'I'm so sorry, my dear. I was going to tell you yesterday, when I phoned, but your father asked me not to,' her aunt said, wiping her hands on a large floral apron. 'He was afraid you wouldn't come if you knew Jack was here, and he just wanted a nice family lunch, with both of you together.'

Nice. There was that word again. 'But you'd rather Jack stayed away? I can tell – why? Don't you like him?'

'Like him? My dear child, I love him as much as your father does. You're forgetting he stayed with me for a few months after all that silly business when he was eleven. So, I know how difficult it is for him to come here, with all the memories this place holds.'

Isy's ears pricked up, as she battled with a reply that wouldn't alert her aunt to the fact that, once again, she didn't have a clue what anyone was talking about.

'But that was a long time ago,' she tried, keeping everything she had crossed.

'It was. It was before he came to live with you in Devon. Quite frankly, I don't know how I'd have coped if it hadn't been for Mrs White.'

'Mrs White?' It was out before Isy could stop herself. And she wished she'd tried a little harder, because it broke the spell of trust between them instantly, that had allowed her a glimpse, however brief, into what had gone before. A world of whispers and innuendos with only the slightest hint of a solid fact.

'Don't go prying into things that don't concern you, my dear,' her aunt was saying. 'If Jack wants to tell you about his past, he will. If he doesn't, let it go. No good will come of it, believe me.'

Isy did but she couldn't disentangle herself now, even if she wanted to. The woman at 48 Osdine Road had promised to contact her if she discovered anything else, and her aunt had just passed on another snippet of information.

Bit by bit, the pieces of Jack's past were gradually coming together. If she tried to wriggle her way out of it now, she might never find her way back. And that wasn't where she wanted to be, left alone in the wilderness. She wanted to help. She wanted to try to find a way to save him, from whatever it was he feared. And she had to do it now, before it was too late, before she vanished from his life forever.

Chapter 15

Jack knew he should be worrying about the week ahead, the bombardment of enquiries for the new fulfilment service they were offering their clients. Or the staffing for the new warehouse in Bristol, but he couldn't. His mind was like a boomerang and it kept coming back to Isy.

'Where are you going?' he'd asked her, once they'd returned from Sussex.

'Out,' she'd replied, heading for the front door. 'Nothing to worry about. Everything's still under perfect control.'

Only he knew it wasn't. That those words alone were guaranteed to give him nightmares, conjuring up a catalogue of disasters, from collapsing tree houses to cartwheels near the cliff. And he was just about to phone her and demand an explanation, with or without menaces, when the house phone started to ring.

'Yes?' he said, picking it up as a number from America flashed up, and the man whose existence he'd spent the last two years cursing, finally had a chance to introduce himself.

'Is Bella there?' Tom asked after the pleasantries had been exchanged. 'She's not responding to my calls.'

To his surprise, Jack had some sympathy with the other guy's predicament. 'She's not the easiest person to get hold of.'

He could hear a slight inhalation of breath of sheer exasperation. 'I need to clarify matters,' Tom said, 'There's been a misunderstanding.'

'There often is with Isy.' Jack still wasn't sure why he was being so pleasant. Or why this guy was divulging so much?

'I shouldn't ask…'

No, you bloody well shouldn't. There, that was more in keeping with how he actually felt.

'But…'

'But you would like me to do the decent thing and tell her you've phoned?'

Tom didn't respond. And it dawned on Jack that this was possibly the first time that Isy's boyfriend had ever seriously considered him as a rival. An observation that was as insulting as it was intriguing. Only now wasn't the time for an in-depth analysis, or a locking of horns. He needed to get hold of Isy himself and ask her what the hell she thought she was up to. But first, he needed her to answer her bloody phone!

Isy wasn't sure what she was expecting when she arrived back from seeing Mrs White. Only finding Jack half asleep on a chair in the hall wasn't one of them. And it was tempting to try to tiptoe past him and pretend she hadn't noticed, when a gust of cold air blew in from behind her and woke him up with a jolt.

'How sweet,' she said, before he could. 'You waited up for me. But I'm home now. You can go to bed.'

'Not so fast.' He pulled himself up to full height. 'I think we need to have a little chat.'

She wanted to resist and tell him that was the last thing that she wanted, but she knew by the tilt of that brow, that wasn't an option. So, having taken off her coat, she followed him, obediently, into the drawing room and waited while he poured them both a whisky.

'OK, then,' she ventured, wondering if he knew where she'd been. 'What have I done this time?' It was as though she were back at school, waiting for her report. *Isy is an excellent scholar but... Isabella has the ability to excel in whatever she chooses but...but... but...but she must concentrate on limiting herself to the task in hand, to not trying to reinvent the wheel when the wheel does not need to be reinvented.*

She could remember it all so clearly. 'Who says?' she'd ask her father. 'If all the great inventors had adopted that attitude, we wouldn't have mobile phones, now would we?'

Her father had not been so impressed. Only Jack had taken her side. He'd commended her for her spirit of defiance, for pushing out those boundaries. The very same boundaries he was about to chastise her for crossing. She could tell by his stance, and the way he was gazing down at her, that she wasn't about to receive this year's prize for innovation.

'I had an interesting phone call this evening with Tom,' he began, watching her sit down on one of the sofas opposite him.

'Tom?' She glanced across and caught his gaze. 'Ah, that Tom.'

'Yes, *that* Tom. He seemed extremely anxious to talk to you and although I don't claim to have his back, I did say I'd pass the message on. Only I couldn't, because, guess what, I couldn't reach you either.'

'And now you want to know where I've been?'

'You took the words right out of my mouth.'

'Don't suppose I can give them back?' she asked, knowing what his answer would be. 'OK then, but promise me you won't be cross?'

'Now how can I do that, if I don't know what you're going to say?'

It was the voice of reason she knew so well. A port in any storm, or so she'd thought. And suddenly the years rolled away, and she wanted to tell Jack everything. What she'd been up to with Mrs White, and her suspicions about Tom. How the man she'd thought she'd loved for the past two years hadn't responded to her call. Someone else had. Someone who sounded ominously like the younger sister of one of his mates. The one with the lisp.

And she wanted to know why the girl was there, in Tom's room, with those lusciously long curls of beautifully blonde hair. Why she'd picked up the phone and not Tom. And why she'd called out to him as though it were the most natural thing in the world, with that unmistakable note of affection.

Isy wanted the answers to all these questions, but she hadn't lingered long enough to ask them, let alone hear the replies. She'd hung up on him and any kind of explanation, because she knew in her heart there wasn't one. At least, not one that was worth waiting for.

So, she centred on something a little more recent, a little closer to home. 'Mrs White, did you know she has a daughter?'

Jack didn't flinch.

'Apparently, she's a counsellor who specialises in child related problems?'

Still Jack didn't flinch, but she could tell she had his attention. Every tightly charged particle of it.

'And your point is?' he asked, eyeing the whisky in his glass.

'Did you know her?'

'I think you know the answer to that.'

'I know, but I want to hear you say it.'

'And I want to know what you think you're doing, discussing my childhood behind my back?'

'Well, I could hardly do it in front of you, now could I?' she retaliated, wondering how he possibly thought she could. 'You won't talk to me. What else did you expect me to do?'

'I didn't expect you to turn into bloody Miss Marple.' He drained the contents of his glass. 'You know, you never cease to amaze me…'

She wasn't sure if she should take that as a compliment.

'…One minute I'm being weighed up by your boyfriend, over the phone. And the next you're digging up my past, like some demented terrier, when I've told you to leave it well alone.'

'You said you wouldn't be cross,' she quickly reminded him, knowing that wasn't strictly true. 'And besides, I'm only trying to help.'

'Well, there's help, Isy. Then there's your definition of the word. Trust me, in my experience, the two are not the same.'

'That's so not true!'

He raised an eyebrow in disbelief. 'Either way, I think I've had enough of this. I'm going to bed.'

'Oh no you're not,' she said, springing up off the sofa before he did. Within seconds she was standing right in front of him. His body, his chest, those muscles, every bit of him was within inches from her. And for a moment, she forgot who she was, who he was, or where they were, and found herself back on that beach, asking him the one question which was troubling her more than any other.

'Why did you send me away?'

'I don't think this is relevant.'

'Oh, but it is. You see, I've spent the last six years pretending it doesn't matter. That you had your reasons. That I didn't need to know. That I didn't care. But I do. I need to know everything because I love you.' And to silence any doubts he might have had, she reached out and traced her fingers gently against his cheek. Thoughtfully, provocatively, across the roughness of his chin, until she felt his fingers find hers. 'Do you still think I'm better off without you?'

She could see the conflict in his eyes, feel the warmth of his flesh, and she knew she should stop pushing him, but she couldn't. She was too tired for common sense. Too frustrated for forward planning. All she wanted was a response, for something in this crazy jumbled up world to make some sort of sense.

'Make love to me,' she said before she could stop herself. 'Because I know you want to.' She could feel him squeeze her hand tightly in his, as though he didn't know what to do next, his mouth so close, so tantalisingly close, but his lips so far away.

'Please, Isy, this isn't fair,' he groaned.

'Isn't it?' She stretched up and kissed him. Tenderly. Longingly.

'Make love to me, like you used to,' she whispered, guiding his fingers down, down, down, to where she wanted them to be. To tease and torment her with the luxury of longing, as he'd done so beautifully before.

'You know I want you,' he said, the words almost catching in his throat, 'that there's nothing I want more than to make love to you. But I can't.'

'Why?' Isy gasped, as he carefully removed his hand from hers. 'Why ever not? If you want to?'

Jack inhaled sharply. 'There's not one bit of you I don't want.'

'Then why won't you? Why won't you make love to me?'

'Because I can't. Because we mustn't. Because you don't want me to – not really.'

She wasn't sure she agreed with that. Her body definitely didn't, but she sensed what he was trying to tell her. And she knew in a world that was far, far away, he was right. That she'd end up hating herself, hating him, hating the universe, for cheating on Tom, because two wrongs didn't make a right, however much she'd hoped they might. She was better than that. Better than Tom. And Jack was better than both of them, even if the expression on his face told her he wished he wasn't. That he would kick himself in the morning, and possibly the rest of his life, for being the better man.

Chapter 16

'You're very quiet this morning,' Jess remarked as Jack swung the van out and onto the M5. 'Don't suppose you want to tell me what's the matter?'

No, he didn't. If he started, he wouldn't be able to stop. And he wasn't in the mood for another heart to heart. He was still reeling from last night's with Isy.

'Forget what I asked,' she'd begged, as she'd kissed him goodnight, her breath warm against his cheek. 'Please, promise me that? That you'll forget everything?'

'Of course I will,' he'd replied, not wishing to upset her any further. 'Forgotten already.' Only it wasn't. How could it be, when he was still aroused by the thought? How could he possibly forget that? Or the ferreting away at his past?

It was impossible. It was like dealing with a rogue missile. You knew it had been primed, but you didn't have a clue where it was going to land. And he didn't want to spend the rest of his life looking over his shoulder. Not anymore. He had to find a way to make it stop. And the only way he could see to do that was to take a giant leap of faith and tell her the truth. Or, at least, what he could and hope she'd leave the rest alone.

So, with his pulse racing, his heart thumping, as though he'd scaled Everest, rather than his inner fears, he'd followed her upstairs. The light was out by the time he reached her bedroom, but the door was still ajar. Pushing it open, he stepped inside. He could see her body turn towards him from under a multitude of blankets, but she didn't try to sit up, or make any attempt at a protest.

And he found himself wondering what she'd do if he sat down beside her and peeled back the bedcovers? Would she offer herself to him, as she'd done less than an hour ago? Would she hold out her arms and, this time, would he accept?

His breathing quickened at the possibilities. A scenario he'd have given his soul to secure. But, first, he needed to tell her a story, just as he had when she was a child.

'Only this time,' he added, sinking down into an old armchair, 'I'd rather you didn't interrupt. In fact, my darling, it's essential you don't. Because I want you to listen to a tale about a boy who suddenly found himself in a world he couldn't control. A world which is a million miles away from the one you know.'

Isy wasn't sure when the tears began to fall. All she knew was she mustn't move. That she must listen in silence to the images he drew, with the briefest of words and very little else, of a boy in ill-fitting pyjamas, who was standing in his sitting room, staring up at two very tall police officers.

Jack blinked. Then he screwed up his eyes tightly. If he couldn't see them, perhaps they couldn't see him? Perhaps they'd all disappear.

Mrs Roberts and the two strangers who were telling him to be brave. Perhaps, when he opened them again, he'd be back with his father, holding onto his jacket. Only this time, he'd never let go.

'You see,' Mrs Roberts was saying, in a room full of clutter, 'he was thinking of you right at the end. He told them where you were.'

She seemed pleased, as though that would provide some comfort. It didn't. Nothing did. He was too young to know what he'd lost, people would say. Only, he knew exactly what he'd lost and what he still had to face.

'I don't want to stay here,' he begged, clutching his book and the bar of chocolate his father had given him. 'Please, don't make me.'

'But your mother…' Mrs Roberts stopped. She was going to say 'will be worried' but they both knew better than that. 'No need to think about that now, eh, young Jack? I'll take you home with me. I'll get my Ted to phone your godfather, Frank, when he comes off his shift, to let him know where you are. I'm sure he's got his number somewhere.'

'Who's Ted,' Isy asked. She'd tried not to move or say anything, but it was impossible. She felt as though her heart would burst.

'Her son. He'd been at school with our fathers.'

'I'm sorry,' she gasped, struggling to sit up, 'I really am, but I can't be quiet, not any more. I need my hankie.' The tears were trickling down her face.

Jack gave a pent-up sigh of pure exasperation. 'This is exactly why I didn't tell you sooner.'

'Why? Because I care about what happened to you?'

'Because I don't want your pity. Your sympathy. Or any other emotion you're about to fling at me.'

'What do you want of me then?'

He pulled himself up out of the chair and back onto his feet, as though he needed time to think. 'I want you, Isy,' he said finally. 'I want you to stop asking questions and to want me for who I am. Who I really am. Not who I was. But how can you? How can you possibly do that when you don't understand what the hell I'm talking about?'

'Then try me,' she cried out at him across the room. 'How do you know if you don't try me?'

'Try you?' He looked as though that was the last thing he wanted to do. His mind, though, was once again back in his past. Only this time it was focussed on one of the police officers. A tall, thin, woman in blue, who held his future in the palm of her hands.

'I'll let his mother know where he is then,' she was saying to Mrs Roberts. 'Once she's had her statement taken.'

'You do that,' Mrs Roberts said, 'no need to get anyone else involved. Folk round here take care of our own. Don't need Social Services intervening, do we?'

Don't we? Jack would ask years later. Maybe not for him. After all, he had this plain-speaking woman and his uncle Frank to fight his corner. But what about the others? Those with no lifeline to cling to when the end finally came?

'What about your uncle?' He could hear Isy's voice, gently prodding. 'What happened to him?'

'Prison.'

'And?'

'And death.' There was no sorrow in his voice. No regret. It was what he deserved for killing his father. 'Some fight inside,' he offered, to fill her thoughts. The man who fucked his mother. What else was there to say?

'And your mother?' she asked, when he wished she wouldn't. 'What did she think she was doing, leaving you all alone – didn't she care?'

He didn't speak. He couldn't. He'd come so far, but he didn't know where to go now. And there was no turning back. No way to erase the past, whether it was five minutes ago, or twenty years. 'I can't do this,' he thought, not aware he'd said it out loud.

'Can't do what?' she asked, throwing her covers off and kneeling on her bed, to face him. 'What can't you do?'

What he'd feared. What he'd kept buried for so long. 'I need to go.'

'No, no, you don't, you can't keep pushing me away.'

He took a few steps back. 'You don't understand.' He studied her face in the half-light. The flickers of concern. 'You think you're helping, but you're not.'

'Yes, yes, I am. You're talking about it and that's good, that has to be good.'

'Good?' The laugh he gave her had a bitter ring to it. 'This isn't some counselling session, Isy. Christ, what do you think I was doing with Mrs White's daughter?'

'But she wasn't me.'

'No, she wasn't. She knew when to bloody stop!' He was lashing out, as he'd done as a child. 'Why won't you leave this alone?' he asked, feeling sick to the core.

'And why won't you talk to me about your mother? Why did you lie to me? Why did you tell me she was dead?'

It was though a lifetime of questions had been launched all at once. He knew he should take shelter, but it was too late for that. 'Why do you want to know?' he asked, in desperation.

'Because she's your mother, Jack.'

'And that should mean something to me, should it?'

'Of course, it should.'

He didn't speak. He couldn't.

'Why do you still refuse to see her?'

'Because…'

'Because?' she queried, gently, as though all he had to do was follow her lead and everything would be all right. 'Because?'

'Because, damn you, I tried to kill her.' There, he'd said it. It was out. The guilt. The shame. A lifetime of hiding. He watched as Isy sunk back down on her bed. 'Is that what you wanted to hear?' he demanded. 'How I almost killed my mother, and would have done, if it hadn't been for your father?'

She opened her mouth, but no sound came.

'Do you feel better now?' He could tell she didn't. That feeling good was the last thing on her mind. 'How is that going to help me?' He willed her to say something. 'And us, Isy? How is that going to help us?'

Still she didn't speak, and it tore his soul in two, the reality of the truth. And he didn't know what to do next. Where to go from here. So, with a howl of frustration he couldn't control, he threw his arms up above his head.

'This is why I didn't tell you,' he managed to get out, the words running ragged in his throat. 'Why I told you you're better off without me.' Then, before he could say or do anything else to destroy them any further, he moved towards the door. This time, though, she didn't try to stop him. Or call him back. Only when he'd reached the hallway, did he turn around to face her.

'The only thing I ever wanted from you was your love. I didn't... don't need your help. Just you. And, from the way you're looking at me now, I doubt I even have that. Not anymore.'

Isy couldn't believe what had happened. Her mind was still in turmoil the following morning, when they rubbed shoulders at breakfast. Each looking at the other, as though they wished they were somewhere else.

'Will you be home this evening?' she managed to ask, watching while Jack grabbed his house keys from the hall table. 'Only I'm thinking of cooking.'

Normally that would have received a swift repost. Jack giving her a thousand reasons why he should stay away to save his stomach, but not today. Not this morning. Probably not ever again, for the rest of their lives.

I'm so sorry, she wanted to say, *for so many things. That I didn't react the way you'd hoped I would last night, that I didn't say or do the things I should have said and done, but it was a shock for me too, as you always knew it would be. And I don't always get things right, any more than you do.*

She wanted to tell him that, to ask him to stop looking at her as though she'd ruined everything they'd ever had, because it wasn't fair. She was trying to save their relationship, not destroy it.

'I'm not sure of my plans,' he said finally.

'I'll make dinner then, just in case. I can always save yours for tomorrow, as a treat.' She attempted a smile, and for a second she thought it had worked, that she saw a spark between them, but then it was gone and so was he.

She wandered back into the kitchen, into the emptiness of what should have been the heart of the home and looked at the list he'd left her. A memo of everything she needed to do this week, from chasing up carpets to the sourcing of staff.

Only three things were missing. She needed to phone Tom, to face whatever it was he wanted to say. Then contact her father and warn him she was intending to pop in later that week. But first she had to reply to the text she'd just received from the lady at 48 Osdine Road.

I've found something which might be of interest.

She knew she should let it go, but she couldn't. Jack had opened his heart to her last night, and he was right. It *was* a world she didn't recognise. A world which was a million miles away from the one she knew, but that didn't stop her from wanting to help him. She just had to work out how. And she needed to do it very carefully, because the last thing she wanted to do now was cause him any more pain.

'It's nearly time to leave. To set off for Devon.'

Only it wasn't Jess's voice that Jack could hear, playing with his thoughts, it was Isy's Aunt Beth's. And he knew, instantly, where he'd gone, when he wasn't watching. He was back in Robertsville, staring up at the kitchen clock, transfixed, as the hands took him slowly, ever so slowly, away from his past.

'You can phone your mother,' the voice was saying, 'and tell her goodbye. I've arranged it with the matron. It's going to be all right.'

Only it wasn't. Jack shook his head emphatically. 'No,' he said. One small word which summed up his whole life to date. All eleven years of it.

'You don't have to, of course you don't have to,' Aunt Beth said quickly. 'No one is going to make you do anything you don't want to do. You know that, don't you?'

No, he didn't. All he knew was that he wanted to punch something, or someone, as he had last week. The aggression bubbling up within him until he wanted to explode. And he waited for the feeling to subside, as he'd been told it would. That it was natural to feel the way he did, and he had nothing to be ashamed of.

Only it didn't feel like that. It felt as though everything was his fault. That he'd killed his father. That he'd tried to kill his mother. That he should have done something more to stop her from destroying herself and turning their house, his world, into a living nightmare, from which there was no escape, no matter what he did.

And, staring up at the clock, he couldn't rid himself of the feeling that none of it would have happened if only he'd been good. If only he'd kept quiet as they'd told him to and given his father a different name. A name that wasn't his uncle Pete's.

'I want it to stop,' he yelled out, as the guilt tore through him, his heart thumping angrily against his ribcage. 'I want it all to stop!'

'And it will, my dear,' Aunt Beth said soothingly. 'It will. Frank will be back shortly to pick you up. You're going to go home with him, as he promised. Everything will be all right.'

He looked across at her. He knew the kindness was well intentioned, even back then, but it didn't change anything. He wanted to shout at her and tell her he'd heard it all before. That he didn't believe anything she said, because nothing ever changed, not in his life. That it was cruel, bloody cruel to make promises you couldn't keep, because it hurt like hell. And all he really wanted was for the pain to stop, and the guilt to go away.

'I never want to see her again,' he said, as though disowning his mother was the simplest thing in the world. 'Can you tell her that from me? That I'm never coming back?'

'Jack?'

'Just do it.'

'Do what?'

'What I say.'

'And what would that be?'

He opened his eyes, in a daze, in a panic. Only to find he was sitting in the van, on the passenger side, and Jess was doing the driving.

'You were asleep,' she said, over the noise of the radio. 'Bad dream?'

'You could say that,' he conceded, pulling out his mobile. 'But it's over.'

Or at least it had been. Until recently, it had been buried at the back of his mind, along with his box. And that, if he'd had anything to do with it, was the way it would have stayed.

*

Patience really wasn't one of Isy's virtues, no matter how hard she tried. And she knew she should wait for Jack to get through the door before she pounced, but she couldn't. She had so many things to tell him, that all thoughts of last night had, temporarily, been swept away in the deluge.

'We have a problem. No, challenge,' she corrected herself as he stood before her in the hall. 'Actually, we've got several of them. Challenges, that is.'

'Has anything good happened since I left this morning?'

She gave the question due consideration. 'My cooking,' she responded with a burst of confidence, not usually associated with her culinary skills. 'Dinner appears to have turned out considerably better than expected. Chicken and chorizo, with some sort of herb concoction from the garden.'

'Nothing poisonous, I hope?'

'Well, I've tasted it and I'm not dead yet.'

The corners of his mouth twitched. 'And the challenges – dare I ask what these are?'

'Tom. He's coming home, two days before Mrs White's party. And he wants to see me.' It was out there in the open before she could stop herself. Only, as Jack's smile vanished and the furrows deepened, she wished she'd kept it hidden just that little bit longer.

'So, that's why he was so keen to talk to you yesterday?'

'That and other things.'

'Such as?' he asked, struggling to take his jacket off.

'Such as we've agreed to meet the day after the party.'

'I see.' Only she could tell he didn't. That he was fumbling in the dark for a way to react to this news, to show her he didn't care, but she could see right through him. And it broke her heart.

'I'm sorry,' she said, knowing there was nothing else she could say. And to prove it, she flung her arms around him and held him close, so close, as though there was nowhere else for them to go.

'Is this a goodbye hug?' he asked with that touch of self-doubt which got to her every single time. 'For what happened last night? Or is this for something else – something you've yet to tell me, perhaps?'

I'm not sure, she wanted to say, *not anymore. I'm so confused*, but this time she kept the words to herself. She was still mulling over her conversation with Tom a few hours earlier. How could she possibly explain that to Jack?

'I missed you,' Tom had said to her from the States. 'Not the same without you, Bella.'

And she'd wanted to yell at him down the phone. To ask him how he had the nerve to do this to her now? To act as though nothing had happened, when their relationship had faltered at the first hurdle, let alone the rest of the course?

'And how is Stephanie?' she made herself ask.

'Stephanie?'

'Eddie's sister – is she coming back with you?'

'She's already back in England.'

'But she was with you, in New York?'

'Do I question what you do, Bella, with your ex?'

'No, but I'm not sleeping with him.'

'Neither am I, Bella. With Stef, that is.'

And part of her wanted to believe him, to know that she'd

177

meant more to Tom than a casual fling that had lasted just over two years. She wanted to ask about the pillows at the flat, with their indentations, the glass she'd found with a distinct rim of red lipstick, not to mention a stray earring behind the cushion on the sofa which wasn't hers.

She wanted to ask why everyone thought they could screw around with her mind, with shadows and lies, but she didn't have the energy. Not anymore.

'I'll be up to London on the Sunday after the party,' she told him. 'I'll see you then.'

'Splendid,' he said, and for one brief moment, she thought he actually meant it.

Chapter 17

'Did you know we've chosen the wrong underlay for the carpets?'

Jack wasn't sure where the 'we' came into it, but he was too much of a gentleman to argue. 'Where exactly are you, Isy?' he asked, those playful tones going straight to his heart, as they always did. 'Only you keep cutting out.'

'I'm driving up to London.'

He took a deep breath. 'It's Thursday. If I'm in Plymouth at the factory and you're not at the Hall, then who the hell is with the fitters?'

'Mrs White.' Jack could almost see the Cheshire cat smile at the other end of the phone.

'Mrs White?'

'Well, Jess is with you and I couldn't think who else to ask.'

'And why, dare I ask, are you driving up to London when it was agreed that you would be around until the weekend?'

'Small challenge,' she said. 'Another one. Senior partner wants me at a meeting with one of our clients. Apparently, I did the original piece of advice, so it makes sense that I carry out the review.'

'And you couldn't refuse the senior partner?'

'Not if I want to keep my job.'

'And you do?'

There was a slight pause which told him all he needed to know. 'Damn it, Isy.' *Damn it to hell.*

'Yes?'

I want you to stay. 'Forget it.'

'I'll try.' She sounded as confused as he felt. 'Whatever 'it' is. And I'm sorry.'

'Sorry?' He took another deep breath, his gut twisting as he braced himself for the possibilities. 'And what, dare I ask, are you sorry for this time?'

'Everything,' she said, and then the line went dead.

If Isy had been aiming for a dramatic exit, she'd succeeded beyond her wildest expectations. She knew she should phone Jack back. That he'd probably be cursing her in every language known to man, but she couldn't, because she still wasn't sure what to say.

She was telling him the truth when she'd said she had to go to London. The senior partner had summoned her, but it wasn't just to see a client, it was to see him too. He wanted to discuss her plans for the future. Would she be able to revert back to full time now Millie had given in her notice?

Isy wasn't sure. She wasn't sure about anything anymore. There were less than four weeks to Christmas. Time was running out. She couldn't afford to be this indecisive. Only how could she tell Jack she was thinking of leaving? Of returning to London for good, when she wasn't sure that was what she wanted herself?

She couldn't. All she knew was that exorcising ghosts came at a price. That he might hate her at the end of it. Despise her. Or worse still, never want to see her again. And then he wouldn't care where she went, just as so long it wasn't here, in Devon, with him.

It wasn't a particularly comforting thought and she was still mulling over the ramifications later that evening, when her father phoned to let her into a secret of his own.

'I never wanted to turn the Hall into a wedding venue, my dear,' he confided. 'To have hundreds of people trampling over your mother's home, but I need the money. I need it even more now, as I can't work at the pace I used to. And I can't ask Jack to keep funding it, out of some sort of misplaced loyalty.'

'Why misplaced?' she asked, trying not to drop food all over Tom's clean worktops. 'Why do you say that?'

She could almost hear his mind struggling with the concepts, let alone his loyalties. And she knew she shouldn't push him, but she didn't have a choice. She needed her father to be honest with her and tell her what he knew. But first, she had a confession of her own. And she needed to make it now, before she changed her mind.

'I've got an address for Jack's mother,' she began tentatively. 'A new one, not the one at Osdine Road, and I'm being sent some notes he wrote to Mrs Roberts by her granddaughter, Samantha. And I know you didn't want me to get involved in any of this, but I'm not six years old anymore. I love him, Dad. I wish I didn't, but I do, and you can't protect both of us for ever.'

She paused to give her father a chance to digest what she'd said, because the last thing she wanted to do was cause him any more stress. Or force him to take sides. Only now she'd started, there was no going back.

'There's more, Dad,' she said, almost wishing there wasn't. 'In the notes, Jack tells Mrs Roberts how his mother is, that she's still 'sick' or she's 'not sick', but in one of them he tells her he's worried because he doesn't know what to do. That he can't contact you, because of some reason or other which Samantha couldn't read, and that he's going to do what he thinks is best, to stop her from ever being sick again. Only I don't think she was sick, not like Mum, and I don't think he tried to murder her.'

She could hear a sharp intake of breath, and she knew she'd finally got her father's attention. 'Did he tell you that?' he asked. 'Did Jack, himself, tell you that he tried to kill her?'

'Yes, yes he did.'

'Then you're right, my dear. It's time we put an end to it. It's time you knew the truth, that we finally tell you what happened that morning when I arrived at Chestnut Lane.'

The same address that Samantha had given Isy over the phone only a few days earlier.

Chapter 18

Christmas was everywhere. Jack couldn't avoid it even if he tried. So, he gave up trying and accepted the fact that his favourite haunt, the Duck and Drake, had been turned into something that would give Isy nightmares for weeks: Santa's grotto for the stylishly challenged, decked out with decorations from the past five decades, all flung together for maximum impact, and very little else.

'Here you are,' he said, handing Mrs White a gin and tonic. 'Here's to you and your help,' he added, raising his own glass of lager to toast the woman who'd saved the day. 'Don't know what we'd have done without you!'

'Ah, Master Jack, you leave that charm of yours for the young'uns. Or Miss Isabella.'

'Don't think it works on her, Mrs W.'

'Don't you be too 'ard on yourself. Or 'er. She didn't 'ave to stay down 'ere with you, now did she?'

He wasn't sure if he agreed with that, but he had no wish to contradict the woman who'd just spent the last two days house-sitting for them.

'Such a shame about 'er mother. Beautiful girl, just like Miss Isabella. Could never sit still, stay in one place, Gawd love 'er, not until she met young Mister Frank. Then there was no going back.'

She gave him a knowing wink over the rim of her wineglass. 'Give 'er time, Master Jack, give 'er time.'

And that was the problem in a nutshell. He didn't know if he had any. He didn't know if he'd have anything at all after tonight.

'She knows.' Those had been Frank's words to him earlier this morning.

At first, he wasn't too concerned. After all, he'd told her about his father and his uncle himself. 'I know,' he said, as he'd turned his attention away from trying to sort out a staff issue for Jess and towards what Frank was trying to tell him. 'We had a conversation – it did not go well.'

'She told me. She also told me that she has an address for your mother. The right address.'

Jack felt as though he'd suddenly been dealt a body blow, that he'd miscalculated a wave and felt the full impact against his chest. 'Please tell me that she's not visited her – for Christ's sake, Frank, please tell me that?'

'It's all right, my lad. She's not done that, but I think she deserves an explanation, don't you, and she's asked that it comes from you.'

The Hall was lit up like a Christmas tree when Isy approached, and she was grateful for the welcome. She was also delighted to see Jack had finished off the drawing room. The curtains she'd chosen now fell majestically against the newly restored oak floor below.

The only thing missing, as usual, was the man himself. Checking her WhatsApp, she found a message lurking among the others. *Phone me when back. I'll get us fish and chips.*

Without thinking, she did what he'd asked, then rushed upstairs. She had half an hour to make sure she was presentable for what might turn out to be the most important meeting of her life.

Jack had rehearsed his speech from the moment he'd known he was giving one. Only the words vanished the moment he caught sight of Isy. She was standing in the kitchen, nervously arranging, and rearranging, the place settings, her figure eminently desirable in a tightly fitting dress, which drew him towards her, as he suspected she knew it would.

And it was tempting to dispense with protocol. To take her in his arms there and then and forget everything. Just for a few precious moments. Only he knew sex wasn't the answer, however much he might wish it was. So, he concentrated on the food instead, and placed the fish and chips he'd bought on the plates provided. Then, opening a bottle of wine, he poured them both a generous measure.

'I should have guessed,' he said, handing her a glass, 'you wouldn't stop. That you'd want to know everything. But I'm not cross,' he added, in case she thought he was, 'because you can't help being you...'

'Thank you.'

'...and I guess you were only doing it because you care about me...'

'Love you,' she corrected.

'Because you love me,' he acknowledged, sitting down opposite her, 'and that by knowing all about me, you still think you can wave a magic wand and make it all right. Well, you can't, Isy, for what it's worth, but I'll tell you about it all the same, since it seems to mean so much to you. And then, when I've finished, I want you to do something for me. I want you to promise that you'll never mention my mother ever again. That I'll never hear another word from you about the woman who lives at 68 Chestnut Lane. Do we have a deal?'

She looked at him from where she was sitting. 'Yes,' she said quietly, 'we do.'

'Good. Then I'll begin…'

It was raining on that last walk home from school. His shoes needed replacing, but wet feet were the least of Jack's problems. All he could feel was the dread. Dread of what he'd find when he got there. Would she be at home? Or would she be out? Would she be alone? Or would she be dead? Because, no matter how many times he'd prepared himself for that eventuality, no matter how many times the doctors kept telling him she wouldn't last another year, she did.

And it wasn't fair, it really wasn't, to build him up and give him hope, then take it away from him. To imagine her gone for good, only for someone to save her, and for it all to start all over again. Because there were only so many times you could believe in miracles. So many times you could pray she'd change, that she'd love you enough to try, to really try to get it right.

He turned into Chestnut Lane. A road of respectability, except for the drunk at no. 68.

The gate squealed on its hinges. Frank had promised to oil it when he was next up. Jack knew he should do it himself, but he had homework and housework, and very little time for anything else.

Putting his key into the lock, he took a deep breath and opened the door. The sickly sweet smell of stale alcohol wrapped itself around his nostrils, but there was no noise. No sound of any music blaring out for the neighbours to moan about; no TV churning out the latest soap. Just an eerie silence. And for a moment he wondered, if maybe… Just maybe… But then he heard a moan, a low pitiful cry for help from upstairs. And deep down, in the very bottom of his gut, he knew the nightmare was back. That it had never gone away, and he'd have to deal with it all over again.

Isy's heart went out to him. Only she knew there was nothing she could say to make it better. So, she watched in silence while he took another mouthful of the wine he'd poured them. Then, without hesitating, she stretched out her hand to him across the table. Their eyes met as he acknowledged the gesture with one of his own.

'I'm not my mother's son,' Jack said, indicating the glass. 'In case you're wondering if I've got her genes, or whatever it is that makes someone like that. Because I haven't and I'm not,' he added, taking her hand in his. 'And you'll just have to trust me on that.'

She did. She trusted him with her life, at that moment. It seemed the very least she could do for everything she was putting him through. So she waited while he gathered his thoughts. Guilt eating away at her, as he prepared himself to go back in time, to bare his soul to the woman he loved. A woman who was hating herself a little more with every word he spoke.

Jack slipped his feet out of his sodden shoes. His socks were soaking, so he dried them with the closest thing he could find – an old jumper thrown at the bottom of the banisters. And he waited, hoping he was wrong about the noise he'd heard. That it was a cat outside. A fox. Anything other than what it was.

And then it began again. He stared up the stairs, at the bridge between life and death, and he knew what he should do. What he'd always done. Phone his godfather. Frank would take care of it. He'd get her taken away to a private rehab which he knew his godfather funded, as they didn't have any money of their own. Only what she got from the Social, and she'd pissed that down the pan before the week was out.

And he shuddered at the thought of what would happen next, when the money ran out. The men who'd slipped and banged their way in and out of the house, giving her more than the cash she'd craved.

He shuddered at the thought of his life so far. The knocks he'd sustained, the bruises he'd hidden, and the ones he'd yet to receive. And he grabbed the house phone and dialled Frank's number. He put his finger over the button to press call. But he couldn't do it. He couldn't summon help. He couldn't do the one thing that would make it stop, because it never did. It never bloody did.

*

'So, what did you do?' Isy asked, wondering for the first time, if what he'd said was true. If he actually had tried to kill his mother.

Jack leant back in his chair. 'What do you want me to tell you?' he asked, staring straight at her. 'What do you want me to say?'

'I want you to tell me the truth.'

'Even if there's no happy ending?'

'Even if there's no happy ending,' she echoed sadly.

'I'll remind you of that when I've finished,' he said, with that all too familiar twist of his lips, 'because this is one story you can't rewrite, however hard you try. And if you try, my dear, darling Isy, you're going to be sorely disappointed, because it won't be the truth.'

Jack didn't know what was worse. Not pressing the button on the phone. Or pressing it and not getting any answer. He tried it several times and each time it went to voicemail. So, he left Frank a message, several messages, before he gave up and forced himself to go upstairs.

His mother was collapsed in the bathroom. She'd knocked her head as she'd fallen. There was blood still trickling down her face and onto the floor beside her.

'I'll get an ambulance,' he said without thinking.

'No,' she shrieked. 'I need a drink. You've got to get me a drink.'

He could only stand and stare at her. The emaciated body of a once beautiful woman, writhing about in agony as she begged him to bring her the one thing she thought she needed that would make it all go away.

189

And, as he stared at her, he knew what he had to do. He grabbed a cleanish towel from the cupboard and ran it under the cold-water tap. Placing it on the gash on her head, he pressed it, as his godfather had told him to do when she'd tried to slit her wrists. He pressed it firmly and all the time she screamed at him to leave her alone and get her a drink. But he wouldn't. And when he'd finished, and the bleeding stopped, he managed to lift her off the floor and half drag her to her bedroom.

Once she was safely slumped on the bed, he went back downstairs and tried the phone again. No answer. He was by himself, and he had to think quick. He didn't know which rehab place she went to and he didn't have any money anyway, so that wasn't going to work. And he knew she hated going to hospital, because they wouldn't let her drink, so he would never get her to agree to that. There was no alcohol in the house that he could see, so he couldn't give her anything even if he wanted to, and he didn't. So, he was left with no other alternative than to improvise, to try to deal with it by himself.

Going into the kitchen, he pulled out an old bucket from under the sink. In it he placed a roll of loo paper, a packet of biscuits, a glass, and an old, slightly rusty thermos flask, which he filled up with water.

He took them upstairs and placed them by her bed. He ignored the language she hurled at him, when she could tell he wasn't going to give her what she wanted. He ignored her pleas, promises, and every other utterance she could devise, his heart thumping loud against his ribcage, as he closed the door behind him and turned the key in the lock.

If rehab didn't work, perhaps this would? Perhaps she'd realise she didn't need a drink after all, if she couldn't have one? Perhaps he'd finally found a way to cure her? The mother of his dreams, and every other boy's reality?

Perhaps he'd finally found a way to make it stop?

'And?' Isy dared to ask, as the silence between them grew. 'What happened next?'

'I nearly killed her.'

'Only you didn't,' she interjected as quickly as she could. 'So that has to be good then, doesn't it?'

Jack didn't look so sure. 'Guilt isn't eased by what you do or don't do,' he said, raising his eyes to meet hers. 'It's about what you're capable of doing. About what you want to do. What you might do again, if you only had the chance. And that scared me, Isy. It scared me shitless.'

'But you didn't kill her,' she persisted, 'you were just trying to save her.'

'Was I?' He gave her a half-hearted smile. 'Or was I just trying to make it stop?'

But she refused to listen to him. 'You were a child, Jack,' she insisted, 'just a child.'

He shook his head. 'I wasn't that innocent. God, if only. I'd lost what little innocence I had by the age of 6, when your father failed to get custody of me. Better off with my mother, apparently. Only I didn't have a clue about withdrawal back then. That she'd go into the equivalent of cold turkey. I just wanted it to end.'

'So, you went for help?' she prompted, squeezing his hand as tightly as she could. *I know you went for help.*

'I wrote to Mrs Roberts,' he acknowledged, returning the gesture. 'She wasn't on the phone so I had to send her a note. But your father turned up the following morning and called for an ambulance himself. And that,' he said, draining the contents of his glass, 'my dear, darling Isy, was that. Not quite the Borgias, but pretty damn close. Murder. Infidelity. Attempted matricide… Rescue… Call it what you will, but it doesn't get away from the fact that I could have killed her. That I'd wanted to, God help me, so many times, and probably would have done if your father hadn't, finally, taken me away.'

But she wasn't having it, not for a single moment. 'Your life was hell, Jack, and you did your best. You did what you thought was right and got the wrong results. Which one of us hasn't done that, at some stage in our lives?' she protested, wondering if he could see the allusions, that she was speaking from bitter experience. 'You never meant to kill her. So, don't you dare go telling me you did, because you haven't got it in you, and I should know that better than most!'

Only he wasn't listening. She could tell his thoughts were a million miles away. That, in his mind, he was being judged, because he was judging himself, and there was nothing she could say to change that. So, she did the only thing she could think of doing. She got up and walked around to where he was sitting. Bending over from behind, she clasped her arms around his shoulders, and gave him an enormous hug. Her cheek resting gently against his hair, while she waited for him to respond.

*

Jack was conscious there was an emptiness in his heart that he'd forgotten existed. One that even Isy couldn't fill, however much he wished she could. Her presence just accentuated the void, and he knew he ought to say something, anything, to fill it. Only he was too worn out for fancy words.

'Thank you,' was all he could manage as he grabbed hold of her hands. 'But if this is pity, Isy, I don't want it.'

'This isn't pity,' she assured him, kissing the hair on his head, 'this is love. I love you, Jack Anthony Mancini, every little bit of you.'

He surveyed the food in front of them. The congealed chips and soggy fish, and he tried to shift his mind from what he'd feared she'd say to what she was actually saying. To grab the future along with her hands, but what if he was wrong? What if he was confusing hope with comfort, as he'd done so many times before?

'Isy...'

'Shush. You don't have to say another word, unless you want to.'

Oh, but he did. He wanted to string sentences together and wrap them around her, like garlands of pearls, with declarations of his love, to show her just how much she meant to him, but he couldn't. Not after what he'd told her tonight. He couldn't take the risk that all this affection, this promise of things to come, was just pity after all. That she'd wake up tomorrow and want nothing more to do with him.

*

Sleep didn't come easily to Isy that night. She lay under a multitude of covers, wishing Jack was there beside her, her mind going over and over everything he'd said, what he hadn't, and what he still had to say.

Why didn't her father try again to adopt him? When he knew of the life he led? Was it because of the death of her mother? Or was it because of her – because she was too young, too demanding, too much of a distraction? Was *she* responsible for his suffering, for Jack's life, before he'd come into hers?

It was the only thing that made any sense. How she'd, unwittingly, confined the man she loved to a childhood of hell. Then, years later, dragged it all up again and made him acknowledge it, in bold, unadulterated technicolour. No wonder he'd rejected her tonight. Her, with her infernal meddling, when she could almost touch the tension, the chemistry sizzling away in their souls.

No wonder he'd got up and walked away, without saying another word. Then closed the door behind him, leaving her alone with the truth, the one thing she'd always thought she wanted. Only now she had it, suddenly, she wasn't so sure. She wasn't sure where either of them went from here.

Chapter 19

The following morning arrived with a fine dusting of snow. It was the first sign of what lay ahead and Isy could have done without it, on top of everything else, because she knew only too well how destructive winter could be. Burst pipes, leaky roofs, and a boiler constantly on the blink.

'I don't suppose Dad has replaced it yet?' she asked, crossing paths with Jack in the hallway. 'The boiler, that is?'

He shook his head. 'Your father resents replacing something which isn't yet broken.'

And are we? she wanted to ask. *Are we broken, after last night? Have I destroyed us for ever?* But she didn't get a chance to pursue it as he appeared to be distracted with a few questions of his own.

'When are you going to London next week?' he asked, sitting down on one of the chairs to lace up his boots.

'On Friday, early. I've got an afternoon meeting. Why do you ask?'

'And you're going to Robertsville the following day?'

Isy nodded. 'To bring Dad home.'

'Good, because I'm coming with you. To London, that is.'

For a moment, she wondered if she'd misheard him. If he'd accidentally got confused and meant Robertsville. So, she asked him. And when he repeated what he'd said, she opened her mouth to protest, but nothing came out.

'I see I've rendered you speechless.' he added with a hint of a smile, but Isy wasn't amused. She felt so responsible for what he was proposing, after last night, and she wasn't sure whether she should be congratulating him or giving herself a very stern talking to.

'Is this such a good idea?' she asked tentatively. 'To come with me to London?'

'Probably not.'

'Then why…'

'Why am I doing it? Because of you, Isy. Because you made me think, and it's a long time since I've done that, since I've allowed my mother anywhere near my thoughts.'

'So that's why you're going – to see her?'

'Possibly. And, no, before you ask, you can't come with me.'

She felt the rejection instantly, and it hurt. 'Are you sure?' she asked as he opened the front door. 'Are you sure you want to do this by yourself?'

'Definitely.'

'And afterwards, when you've seen her, will you stay with me?'

'At Tom's? I don't think so.'

'You've got it all worked out, haven't you?' Only he hadn't. She could hear it in his voice, see it in his eyes, in that glint of reckless determination, that he hadn't got a clue. He was winging it, as he did on the bike or on the waves, whenever he felt the forces were against him.

But she knew, as he slammed the front door shut, that there was no way she was going to allow him to do any of this by himself. Any more than she had three months ago, when he'd asked her to stay and help with the house.

Jack might think he'd cut the cord which bound them, that he was master of his own destiny. But it would take considerably more than one act of ill-conceived defiance to stop Isy. And if he didn't know that by now, then he really didn't know her at all.

'The only way to get past the pain, my lad, is to throw everything you've got into the gap, and hope it works, that it paves the way to the future.' It was one of Frank's favourite sayings and Jack had taken it to heart when Isy had left him the first time. He'd thrown himself into his work, in the belief it might work, that he wouldn't go mad.

Only he wasn't sure it would work a second time. And he knew he couldn't take the risk. His head was telling him one thing, that he really couldn't spare the time. But his heart was playing for a different prize here, Isy, and he had no intention of losing her again, even if it cost him far more than she'd ever know.

'Mrs White's cake…'

'What?' Her words brought him back to where he was with a jolt, trying to work out how to balance an increase in orders with a lack of supply.

'She's pregnant.'

'What, Mrs White?' he asked, looking up at her from his desk in the study.

'No, idiot, Minnie from Made to Perfection. She's gone into

premature labour and they're keeping her in until God knows when. And don't you dare make some wisecrack about the name of the business or buns in the oven, because I promise you, I'm not in the mood. I've just had an email from a client who's impossible to deal with, and now this!'

He wanted to burst out laughing, if only to defuse the tension he could feel emanating towards him.

'Sit down, Isy.'

'I haven't got time.'

'Yes, you have.' He indicated her father's chair. 'Now tell me again, what's the deal with the cake?'

When Isy had finished, she felt such a fool. Of course, there was a solution. There was always a solution. In this case, there was his mate, Matt, at The King's Head. He would know someone who could make a cake. A replica of a fairy castle, with a picture of Elvis on the side.

'Elvis? Mrs White?' Isy had queried. 'Are you sure you want Elvis?'

'Keep the old man 'appy, Miss Isabella. And Gawd knows, you need to keep the menfolk 'appy.'

Isy still wasn't sure if she agreed with that, but she could have kissed Jack all the same, because Matt did know of someone. A baker who could help out in the time frame. So, cake problem solved. It was a shame she couldn't say the same about everything else.

Chapter 20

It was over twenty years since Jack had left London with Frank. Yet, as Isy drove him back into the metropolis, he felt as though he'd never been away. His gut tightening with every mile they covered, while she dodged the traffic and headed straight for Battersea.

'Tell me again why you didn't come on the bike?' she prompted, once she'd parked the Mini safely underground.

'Problem with the clutch. Need to fix it.'

She didn't look convinced and he didn't blame her. The clutch was fine. He just didn't want to tarnish his wheels with what he was about to do. Any more than he'd let Isy anywhere near Chestnut Lane.

'Are you sure you don't want to come up?' she asked, indicating the block of flats behind her.

He glanced across at the building. It was a template for modern living, but he had no desire to take his exploration any further. The last thing he wanted to do was step into Tom's world, if only for a few minutes.

'I've booked a room at the B&B down the road,' he said. 'I should be getting off.'

Yet still he stayed where he was, his feet firmly fixed to the pavement. And he could tell Isy was hesitating too, dressed as she was for the Arctic, in her woolly hat and matching gloves. That she was still trying to find the words to ask him if he really wanted to do this by himself.

He didn't, but he sure as hell wasn't going to tell her that. Nor was he going to take her with him, especially after what Frank had told him last night.

'She's not so good, my lad, I'm afraid. Her pancreas, I suspect.'

'Does she know I'm coming?'

'She won't seek help until you do.'

Jack could only guess at the reason why, but he wouldn't disappoint her. Not now he'd come so far. Yet still he remained where he was, staring across at Isy, as though she was the only thing in his life that made any sense.

'We'll have dinner, when I'm back,' he said, as though that gave them something to aim for. 'I won't be late.'

'Promise me? Promise me you'll keep in touch?'

He couldn't help but smile. 'I'm going to Hammersmith, Isy, not bloody war.'

'I know. It's just I could have come with you.' The sense of sadness so strong, so mind-blowingly poignant, that he knew he was doomed before he drew another breath.

'Come here,' he said, holding his arms out to her as he'd done so many times before.

'United against the world?' Those were the words he remembered. The words she'd spoken to him that night in Sheffield. 'Whatever happens, you'll always be there for me, won't you?'

Only he hadn't been. He'd let her down when she'd needed him the most. And it would serve him bloody well right if she did the same thing to him right now. If she left him to face his demons by himself. His heart set to plummet just seconds before she answered his call. Her arms wrapped tightly around his chest. Her bobble hat tickling his chin, provoking him, until he knew what he had to do. He had to see her face. Feel her lips, touch her tongue, and know that he was loved, if only for the very last time.

'Jack?' she queried, when he tilted her chin and looked straight into her eyes, but she didn't resist. She returned the gesture with more passion than he was expecting, more enthusiasm than he could ever have hoped for. A long, luxuriously licentious kiss teasing every part of his anatomy, until finally he knew he had to break away.

Perhaps he was going into battle after all? Perhaps he was making a statement outside his rival's flat? Some animalistic instinct to claim what was rightfully his? Or maybe it was simply because he loved her more than life itself? And he wanted her to know that? That whatever happened next, it wasn't her fault, it was his. And how, thanks to her, he finally had a chance to try to put things right.

Isy was struggling to concentrate on what her client was saying, but her mind was all over the place.

'So, we're all agreed, are we?' an elegant woman in a pencil skirt suit was asking. 'You can get a draft heads of terms out to us by Wednesday?'

She nodded, wondering if her client had any idea how difficult it was to arrange for special diets so close to an event? Or find gold balloons with Elvis on? Probably not. Not an everyday occurrence in the corridors of power.

'I'll get them checked off by a partner and have them with you by Wednesday latest,' she promised. *Just please don't ask me how.*

Now, though, she needed to concentrate on Jack. The man who'd promised to contact her once he'd finished doing whatever it was he was doing. Seeing his mother. Sorting out his past. She wasn't entirely sure what, but she knew she had to be good and contain her curiosity, even if it was playing havoc with her concentration.

So, she waited as the hours passed slowly by, and still no message arrived. Her fingers itching to pick up her mobile and try his, even though she knew that was pointless.

'I'm switching my phone off,' he'd said as he kissed her goodbye. And she had no reason to doubt that he'd phone as he'd promised, but she was worried. So worried she almost dropped the mug of coffee she was holding when her mobile finally rang.

'Yes?' she gasped, picking it up without thinking it could be anyone else but Jack. And when it wasn't, she didn't know if she was relieved or disappointed. 'Tomorrow, Dad,' she heard herself say, 'we'll be down to take you home tomorrow. But now I have to get back to work.'

Only she couldn't. The agreement was a mixture of words she couldn't compute into anything nearing comprehension. And when Jack finally phoned, she felt as though her whole future pivoted precariously on that small piece of buzzing plastic.

'Jack?' she cried in delight. 'It's you!'

'Of course, it's me.'

'I've been so worried. Where the hell are you? It's late. It's after eleven. Are you OK? Is everything…'

'Isy.' She could hear the command in his voice, against the tiredness. 'Can you shut up for a moment and listen? I'm at the hospital.'

It was what she'd feared. He'd killed her. She'd killed him. No, that was nonsense. He was talking to her. But she could have attacked him? Or him her? Or both each other? The possibilities were endless, but she wasn't leaving him to face this alone. 'I'm coming…'

'No. No, you're not.'

'Yes. Yes, I am.' She switched the mobile onto speakerphone. 'Already putting boots on,' she shouted across the room at him. 'So just stay where you are!'

There was a silence and she thought she'd lost him, that he'd cut her off completely. 'Jack?' she gasped, grabbing the phone as though it were the very essence of life itself.

'I'm here.'

'Thank God for that.'

'I was just wondering how the hell you're planning to find me, if you don't actually know where I am?'

St Cuthbert's Hospital, just five miles away. Isy threw everything she could think of, including her satnav, into her bag and dashed down to the underground car park to retrieve her Mini, her mind toying tirelessly with the questions she'd never had a chance to ask.

'Got to go,' he'd said. 'Text me when you're here. I'll meet you outside.'

So, she did. She paid the exorbitant parking fee the local council requested and waited in the dark. Hints of Christmas passed her by, with promises of the festivities ahead. But not for her. Not for the poor souls inside. And certainly not for the man coming towards her.

Jack looked so tired, his whole physique exuding exhaustion as he waited for her in the doorway, his jacket clasped loosely between his hands. And before he had a chance to even acknowledge her presence, she went up and gave him the biggest hug she could manage.

'You're OK,' she muttered, raising her face to meet his. 'You're not hurt?' She searched his eyes, frantically trying to get some idea as to what might have happened.

'What exactly were you expecting?' he asked, giving her a quizzical glance all of his own.

'You know me – I have a vivid imagination.'

'That's what's worrying me,' he admitted, with a sigh of weary resignation. 'Shall we go inside and get a coffee?'

She stepped back and slipped her arm through his. It was going to be another long night, she could tell. And although he'd never say it, she knew he was glad she'd come.

Jack stared at the buttons on the vending machine. All he had to do was press them to get what he wanted. A bit like that button on the phone all those years ago. Only he couldn't. His mind was too busy trying to assimilate everything that had happened.

It was only when Isy passed him a beaker of his own, that he felt his brain engage.

'Do you want to talk about it?' she prompted, as they sat down at a table in the corner.

'I don't know.' And he didn't. Eight hours earlier, things had been different. He had known exactly what he was doing. He was facing the future by, finally, trying to acknowledge the past. But now he wasn't sure what to think. He was sitting in a deserted café, in the middle of the night, with his plans in tatters around his feet. Trying to be strong, but too tired to work out what that was, or how the hell to make things right.

'So, you've come back, have you?' Those were the first words his mother had said to him in over twenty years. And he knew he should say something back, but he couldn't. Nothing seemed appropriate, adequate, or even vaguely real.

'You always was a quiet one,' she acknowledged, leaning back heavily on a stick. 'Suppose you'd better come in then.'

He fought the offer, every bone in his body jarring at the possibilities. The memory of the sodden shoes… The locked door… Her screaming… The ambulance men and the deathly pallor of the woman who was turning around to face him. Her eyes penetrating his, as they always had, screwing up his insides with demands he couldn't meet.

'I almost killed you,' he said before he could stop himself. 'I wanted to.'

'Well, you didn't, did you?' she retaliated with that raspy laugh he'd tried so hard to forget. 'Now, are you going to stop bleating about the bleeding past and come in or what? I bought cake, special like.'

Jack could still feel the disbelief, the anger simmering away inside. 'She'd never bought me anything in my entire life,' he told Isy, 'and she got me cake. Would you believe it? Bloody cake!'

Isy looked at him as though she didn't know how to respond. And he knew he wasn't making it easy for her, but then he was having a hell of a job sanitising it for himself.

'Did you go in?' she asked tentatively.

'Did I go in?' He closed his eyes, wondering what would have happened if he hadn't. If he'd walked away, rather than stepped into what once was his home, waiting and watching as the door closed slowly behind him.

'I know,' his mother said before he did. 'Bleeding mess, ain't it, but I've not been that good lately.'

You never were, Jack wanted to add, *or sober enough.* Yet she appeared remarkably sober today. And he'd forgotten what an accomplished actress she could be when she'd wanted to convince someone she was the perfect mother. He'd forgotten the highs and lows, the hopes and fears. How he just wanted to turn around and walk back out before it all came flooding back and consumed every ounce of energy he'd ever possessed.

'I can't stay long,' he said.

'Got someone waiting for you, have you?'

'No,' was the word which came out.

'Shame,' she said, sinking down awkwardly into a chair, 'you're a good-looking boy. Now go and put the kettle on and we'll have tea.'

'Tea?' Isy queried.

'Yes, tea. She'd laid out a tray with two cups and saucers, sugar cubes and milk. And beside it was the cake…chocolate, before you ask.'

'Your favourite.'

'How the hell did she know that?'

Isy didn't know. She was feeling her way through this like a skater on thin ice. Terrified she might do or say the wrong thing, which would cause the veneer to crack.

'So, where is she now?' she asked, as gently as she could.

'Intensive Care. They've sedated her. Her pancreas, it's shot.'

Isy wasn't quite sure what he meant, but it didn't sound good. 'I can come with you, if you like, to sit with her? To keep you company, when we've finished our coffees?'

He looked confused. 'And why would you want to do that?'

Because I love you? Because she's your mother? Because it's my fault you're here? Only she didn't say any of it. She could tell he wasn't listening. That he was back with his memories, and she needed him to take her there too.

Jack poured his mother a cup of tea. That way he knew most of it would end up in the cup rather than the saucer. He cut her a piece of cake and passed it to her. He could see she was in pain and struggling to hold herself together for him. And he wanted to say he was sorry, but he wasn't sure what he was apologising for and, if he started, where it would all end. So, he kept quiet and sat down opposite her, on the same sofa he'd slept on all those years ago at Osdine Road.

'A good man, your uncle Frank,' she rasped. 'He did us proud.'

He raised a quizzical eyebrow.

'He bought you up proper, didn't he? And kept me here, safe like. Paid for this house. Paid for my care.'

Only it didn't cure you, did it? It didn't save you. The words at the forefront of his mind, only he didn't voice them. What was the point?

'I'm dying Jackie.'

Her voice broke the silence, but he'd heard it all before.

'When Frank phoned, said what you was going to do, do you know what I thought?'

He shook his head, waiting for an outburst which never came.

'I thought, God, he's gone and done it, he's answered me bleeding prayers.'

'But you don't believe in God?'

'Do now, Jackie, bleeding do now.'

And, in spite of everything, he found himself smiling.

'You see,' she said, 'we're going to do what proper families do. We're going to have tea together. And then, when you're done with me… When you've said what it was you wanted to say, you can get us a bleeding ambulance.'

Isy stared across at Jack in the silence of the café. She knew she ought to ask him what happened next, but she was still digesting what he'd already said. One bit in particular was going around and round in her brain. 'So, Dad bought the house for you? The house she's living in?'

He met her gaze and she could sense his guilt. 'I didn't know it back then. I just thought he paid our rent. I didn't know he'd raised a mortgage on the Hall to buy it outright. I didn't know any of it until I started earning and asked to help, to take over the rental payments. To refund her rehab.'

'I see,' she said, as certain things finally began to make sense. 'So that's why you're paying for all of this. Sorry, *lending* Dad the money for the renovation. It's because his money's been tied up elsewhere. What a mess.'

'I know, and if I could change it, I would. You know I would.'

'I know,' she said, touched by the concern in his voice that she could think anything else. 'I know you wouldn't do anything to hurt my father, but I do think you should see your mother before we go,' she added, bringing the conversation back to where it had all begun. 'I know what you're thinking, that you've been here before but what if you're wrong this time? What if she doesn't pull through?'

'She will.'

'You don't know that.'

'She's done it before, Isy. She's done it so many times before.'

The emptiness, fear, and resistance were all there in his face and in every gesture he made, all wrapped up in denial. And she knew she mustn't push. That there were some bridges you couldn't cross, no matter who you were, or how much you wanted to help.

Jack watched as his mother sipped her tea. She was fighting off the spasms of withdrawal, and he wished he could find a way to try to alleviate them, just as he had before he'd left. To suggest a solution when they both knew there wasn't one to be had.

'I can get you an ambulance now,' he offered, as his mother almost bent over double in her chair. 'You don't have to wait.'

'No,' she grimaced, straightening up. 'You've not come all this way to see me die. You came to talk to me. So bleeding talk to me.'

Only he couldn't. Not now he was here. All the questions he'd wanted to ask, of why this, why that, and why the other, disappeared. In their place was an overwhelming sense of loss for the things they'd never know, let alone share.

I can't do this, he thought. *I can't talk to you as I'd planned, because you're incapable of providing the answers. If you could, none of this would ever have happened.* And to his surprise, he began to talk to her about himself. About all the things he'd sworn he'd never tell her. To try to give her an insight into the life of the son she'd never really known.

And when he'd finished, she asked him again, 'Is there someone special in your life, Jackie? Someone to make all the pain go away?'

He wasn't sure if Isy qualified as a remedy for pain, as she'd caused more than her fair share of it over the years, but she was special.

'Of course, you don't have to tell me.'

No, he didn't, but he found himself doing so all the same.

'So, Frank's little girl, eh?' she said with a nod of approval. Then, with a gesture he wasn't expecting, she put her hand into the pocket of a wine-stained cardigan and pulled out a box.

'Ain't no use to me no more. It's yours.'

He was all ready to refuse it, to tell her what she could do with the gifts she kept offering, but he wasn't a cruel man. So, he took the dilapidated box from her and opened it. Inside there was a small ring, a sapphire with a diamond either side. A token of love, given a lifetime ago, when there was still hope.

'He deserved better than me,' she said.

'He did.'

'So did you.'

There was a raw honesty in her voice that he'd never heard before. And he wanted to answer it in the same vein and let her know he had regrets too. That he'd allowed his anger to fuel his hate, his guilt to feed his intransigence. And, if it wasn't for Isy, he'd have continued to do so, but he'd said too much already.

So, instead, he switched on his mobile and called for an ambulance. He waited until they arrived, as he'd done so many times before. Only, this time he went with her to the hospital. And when she held out her hand, to thank him, he almost took it.

Chapter 21

It was a long drive down to Devon the following day. Isy could see her father glancing at them from the back of the Mini, as though he'd been thrown into a foreign film without the benefit of subtitles.

'Have you two fallen out, my dear?' he queried, as soon as Jack disappeared to pay for the petrol. 'Only you've hardly spoken to each other since we left your aunt's.'

The words were so kindly spoken that she wanted to break down and tell him everything, but she couldn't. They'd only just passed Sevenoaks and she had over 200 more miles to drive before she could even begin to try to explain what had happened last night.

'Would you like me to come in with you?' she'd asked Jack, once she'd pulled up outside the B&B. 'I can park the car at Tom's and walk back?'

'No.'

'No to me walking back or coming up?'

'No to both.'

There was no attempt at clarification, and she knew she should leave it after everything he'd been through, but she couldn't.

It was the second time in less than two weeks he'd rejected her, and it hurt.

'Are you sure?' she asked, willing him to change his mind. 'Are you quite, quite sure?'

He turned his head towards her. A flash of light from a nearby lamp illuminated his face in the gloom, and she could see the look in his eyes. One of wounded pride, tinged with despair, and it cut her heart in two.

'It's all right,' she managed to croak. 'I won't ask again.'

'Isy...'

'No need to explain. Probably better this way, anyway, what with Dad, the party, and Tom.'

Tom. Shit. As soon as the word left her lips, she regretted it, because she could sense Jack's withdrawal, long before he'd left the car.

'I'll tell you about it when we're home, Dad,' she sighed, watching Jack pay for the petrol.

'And the job?' her father asked. 'Have you made up your mind about that?'

'I think I'll take it. I think it would be better for everyone if I went back to London, and I only came down for the weddings.'

Her father looked at her anxiously. 'Have you told Jack about this yet – what you're thinking of doing?'

She shook her head. 'Not with everything that's going on at the moment, with the party and his mother.' She owed him that much at least. Or at least she thought she did. After last night, she wasn't so sure. She didn't think he'd care where she went, just so long as she wasn't here with him.

213

*

Jack was beginning to think the unthinkable. He had ever since he'd left the hospital, when he'd realised he was back to where he'd been six years ago. That he was living in a fool's paradise if he thought Isy would want him now. Now she'd seen the reality. She deserved something – someone – better. She always had. It was why he'd sent her away in the first place; to find happiness in London, in a world full of Toms. He couldn't compete with that, even if he wanted to, and he didn't. He was who he was. It just wasn't good enough for Isy.

'I'm going for a run,' he said, when he caught up with her the following morning. She was sitting in the kitchen in the Hall, huddled over her laptop, wearing more layers than he could count.

'But it's still dark… And it's freezing?' she queried, looking at him as though he was mad. But it was more than that. He could see it in her eyes, and it froze his heart faster than the weather outside ever could.

'The checklist for the week is in the study,' he managed to say. 'Don't be put off by the length. I've tried to include everything.'

She gave him a glimmer of a smile. 'Don't you ever sleep?'

He returned the gesture with an attempt of his own. 'I will when it's over. The party,' he clarified, in case she'd misunderstood. *And you,* he wanted to ask, *what will you do when it's over?* Only he couldn't bear to hear her response. So, he did what he'd always done when the pain began to bite. He kicked his imagination into touch by focussing on the practical. Saturday, at three o'clock, when the Hall would be full of guests. The fruition of two years of bloody hard graft.

'You've done me proud, both of you,' Frank had told them

214

yesterday, admiring the fresh tones of the walls around him: hues of apricot in the main drawing room contrasted in mood with the richness of the crimson red paper in the dining room; the chinoiserie in the four bedrooms, already completed, with the warmth of wall to wall carpeting for those unslippered feet. 'Couldn't have done it better myself.'

Jack could still feel the surge of pride, and he wanted to share it with Isy. He wanted to acknowledge her part in getting the Hall to where it was today, because he couldn't have done it without her. But it was difficult to talk to someone who was doing their best to avoid you. And who now was looking at you as though you were out of your mind.

'Jack…?' she queried, as he picked up his mobile.

'Yes?'

She hesitated and he willed her to say something, anything, so he could at least have some idea what he was up against. Then, when she didn't, when she went back to answering her emails, he set off into the darkness, wondering if she knew just how devastating nothing could be.

I love you. Those were the words Isy had wanted to say. *I love you so much, but I can't do this anymore. I've destroyed everything and I'm going back to London before I make it a thousand times worse.*

It all seemed so simple in her mind. Only the speech died on her tongue every time she tried to voice it. And it was so unlike her to hold back, but she was so scared of the finality of what she had to say. Because she knew that once spoken there'd be no way back for either of them.

'I'm going to have a shower,' Jack announced on his return from his run.

She peered up at him from what she was doing, opening Christmas cards in the hallway.

'Dad's gone to Jess's for breakfast,' she said, before he could ask. 'And your mother's still the same. Dad phoned.'

He gave her a nod in acknowledgement, his whole physique exuding a heady cocktail of pumped up masculinity and perspiration, and it was all Isy could do not to ask to join him. To slip into the shower beside him, and allow herself to be seduced by just the thought of what might happen next. Their bodies, warm, wet and wonderfully aroused, rising in a rhythm all of their own, in such delicious harmony, until neither of them could wait, or control that moment – the sheer exhilaration of love.

And, before she knew it, she found herself following him up the stairs, turning right instead of left. Going along his corridor, not hers, until she came to a halt outside his bathroom. She could hear the pump, the spray of water splashing against the tiles, but she didn't go in. She didn't allow herself the luxury of sight. Instead, she wandered into his bedroom, and positioned herself, cross-legged, in the middle of his bed.

The curtains were open. Outside, daylight had broken through. Inside, the heating was struggling to make a similar impact. Shivering, she drew his duvet up around her for warmth as well as comfort.

'You could have been a Spartan,' she remarked when he finally appeared. 'Doesn't your radiator work?'

'And you'd have done well in *Aladdin*. Only I wasn't aware I'd summoned you?' He stood before her with just a towel wrapped around his waist. 'Or that I'd added my bedroom to the checklist for the week?'

But she wasn't listening. She was looking at his chest, glistening with a freshness and a fully toned appeal that was impossible to ignore. The aroma of shower gel, gently refreshed the room with a fragrance all of its own. And his arms, which once had held her so secure, were unfettered by clothes. Jess's words coming back to her, as she threw herself off the bed and went to where he was standing.

'Don't,' she implored, as he attempted to divert her by grabbing a shirt off the front of his wardrobe. 'Please don't fight me, not now, not after everything?'

To her surprise, he relented. He allowed her to draw his left arm towards her, so she could examine the mixture of scars and waxen skin that engulfed the outer side. A patchwork of destruction, as he'd battled to defend himself against the crowbar which had broken the bone beneath.

'Not my finest hour,' he acknowledged, but he didn't resist. He didn't try to shake her away, the touch of her hand, the feel of her fingers, as they explored the paths twisted in his flesh.

'I'm sorry,' she said, 'I'm so sorry.'

'Don't be. It served a purpose.'

'I wasn't talking about Jess.' She looked up into his eyes and she could see the question he didn't dare ask, so she answered it for him. 'I'm leaving.'

'I see.' He cleared his throat and took a few steps back, as though

217

she'd hit him with her fists rather than her voice. 'And…and just for the record, is this before the party or after?'

'After, off course. Do you really think I would leave you all before it?'

He looked as though he wasn't sure. As though he didn't know what she might do to him anymore, but it was only for a moment. 'Thank you,' he said, retrieving his shirt and yanking it on unceremoniously, 'for letting me know.'

They could have been discussing the weather, rather than their lives, and she wanted to yell at him for being so dismissive, for not even trying to change her mind. 'Is that all you have to say?' she asked.

'What do you want me to say? That you should stay? That you should give up everything you've worked so hard for and live the rest of your life with a guy like me?'

Yes! She wanted to scream, but he wasn't interested. He was too busy grappling with the buttons on his shirt.

'I think you should go,' he said, when he'd finally finished.

'You do?'

'Yes, I do.'

She caught the glint in his eyes, and it scared her, because she'd seen it once before. 'You're right,' she said, as he began to rummage in his drawers for some boxers. 'I should go. I'll leave on Sunday. I'll stay with Tom until I can find somewhere else to live.'

'And why would you do that?' he asked, turning back to face her. 'Why would you need to find somewhere else to stay?'

'Because I think Tom's cheating on me. No, I know he's cheating on me. I just need to prove it.'

'But what if you're wrong, Isy? What if you've done the usual and put two and two together and got six?'

She knew she should be insulted by his lack of faith, let alone his insinuation that she couldn't add up, but this wasn't the moment. She had something else to tell him, and she needed to tell him now, before she lost her nerve completely.

'I'm so sorry about your mother, Jack. About your family, about forcing you into something you never wanted to do. I should have listened to what everyone was telling me. What you were trying to tell me. I should have left it all alone.'

This time, though, she didn't wait for him to reply. She turned and headed for the door.

'What you did was a good thing, Isy.'

His words didn't register at first. All she could hear was the pumping of her heart and a desperate plea for dignity, buried somewhere deep at the back of her brain. It was only when she felt his hand against her arm, pulling her back towards him, that she allowed herself to turn around and face him.

'Are you sure about Tom?' he asked, his eyes searching hers with an urgency she wasn't expecting.

She nodded. 'There was a picture on Facebook, a photo of them in New York when Tom said Stephanie was in England.'

'And,' he asked hesitantly, 'how do you feel about that?'

How did she feel about that? About the betrayal? Hurt? Angry? Relieved? How could she tell Jack that? That she was actually relieved to find that Tom had cheated on her? That she had the chance to break it off? To assuage her guilt of loving someone else? Of loving him?

'I'm a disaster,' she muttered, more to herself than to him. 'A walking disaster.'

'I wouldn't say that.'

'Wouldn't you?'

'More like a series of mini disasters.'

She smiled, wondering if he knew just how much she wanted him to kiss her. To wrap her up in that freshly showered body of his and make all the agonies of the past few months go away, until there was nothing left but them.

'Do you still want me to go – to London?' she asked.

He looked as though he wasn't sure, his mind sifting through a lifetime of experiences in just a few seconds. And she knew he wanted what she did, that she was mad to even doubt it, but she just needed him to say it.

'Jack?' she prompted, when he didn't.

'I think you should go,' he said finally, 'while you can. I think it will be for the best.' And she knew the words were causing him pain. She could hear it in his voice, see it in his eyes, the inflection in his cheeks, but it was nothing to what she was experiencing.

'If that's what you want,' she made herself say, with more courage than she knew she possessed. And with her head held high, she forced herself to turn her back on him, for the second time in her life.

Chapter 22

'What time are the agency staff coming?' Frank asked, wandering into the dining room to join his daughter.

'Twelve, midday, Dad. In three hours' time. And, yes, they'll have a uniform and know what is expected of them, but I'll run through it again, in case anything has been missed.'

'Good.'

'And Jack's in the study, with Jess,' she said before he could ask. 'Sorting out ballasts for the balloons, so we can put them in the middle of the tables. Balloons with Elvis on.'

She still couldn't get her head around the concept, but at least the information seemed to pacify her father.

'Never thought we'd hold a party for sixty in this house, my dear, let alone fit all the tables in here.'

'In the summer, we'll get a marquee and do 100,' she assured him. 'It's just the winter when we need to have smaller gatherings inside.'

'Or not have any at all?'

She was dismayed at the note of wishful thinking in her father's voice. He'd almost killed himself for something he didn't really

221

want. And she knew she ought to try to find a solution for this as she did for everything else, but she was too exhausted to think about anything which wasn't on her schedule.

She'd been up before Jack this morning, arranging flowers, laying out the china, the glasses, and preparing everything she could before the caterers arrived at one. At two, she'd go and get herself changed in time for the Whites' arrival. And then, at three, if everything went according to plan, the guests would start to arrive.

'What sort of music are we having?' her father was asking. 'What about the music?'

'One of Jack's mates has put together a medley of the tunes they wanted. Anything from the big bands to Madonna, and – before you ask – no I don't know why Madonna. And Harry's set it to coincide with an array of photos flashing up on the screen in the second drawing room.'

'Good.'

'So, you see, Dad, you really can stop worrying. It's going to be just fine. I promise you. Just fine.'

Jack was trying to work out how he'd got himself involved with attaching pieces of string to fishing weights. 'Next year, we're going to do this properly,' he said, as the knot he was trying to tie came undone again. 'We're going to need proper ballasts.'

'I'm sure no one will notice, not today,' Jess said soothingly. 'And we can hide them with a little of this gold tissue paper. Look,' she said, smothering the base with a hastily but craftily constructed rosette. 'Neat, eh?'

He attempted a smile, but it petered out somewhere in transmission.

'When's Isy leaving?' Jess asked. Then, when he didn't respond, 'Look, I know you don't want to talk about it, but it's still going to happen whether you face it or not.'

Jack was only too aware of that. In just under twenty-four hours it would all be over, and she'd be gone. That, once again, he'd done the decent thing and set her free, and he should be feeling really good about it, but he wasn't. He was feeling like crap. As though he'd performed some sort of masochistic torture, which had sucked out his soul and left a vacuum in its place.

And the only way he could get through it this time was to pretend it wasn't happening. That it had never happened. Just as he had when she'd left him the first time.

'How's your mother?' Jess asked, as though she knew she had to change his thoughts.

'No worse.'

'That's good then, isn't it?'

Was it? He wasn't sure anymore. All he knew was that when this was over, he was going to need a lifetime's worth of self-analysis, and a bloody good cure for the pain.

'Don't suppose you could help me with this hook?' Isy's voice drifted down the stairs towards him. 'Only Dad's tried but his hands keep shaking.'

Jack took in the vision before him, and suddenly he was back to where he'd been over twenty years ago. Standing at the bottom of the staircase, while she'd cascaded down the banisters towards

223

him. Such energy. Such excitement. Such enthusiasm for life.

'No pirates this time,' he said with a nod to the past.

She stared up at him and smiled. 'I often wonder how you'd have looked in those earrings.'

She turned around in trusting anticipation. Her hands brushing her hair away from the back of her neck, so he could reach the clasp. And it was all he could do not to kiss that sudden exposure of flesh, to lower his head and claim her for his own.

'New perfume?' he asked in an attempt to steady his nerves, his hands, and everything else, as he tried to touch the piece of wire and not her.

'You noticed?'

I notice everything about you, he wanted to say. *Every tiny detail.* Instead, he concentrated on drawing the hook and eye together. His brain struggling to dismiss what his eyes could not, the pleasing contours of the woman before him, the folds of the tightly fitting piece of material, all in emerald green, as they fell seductively over her hips, towards the silken sheen of her legs.

'There,' he said. Or, at least, he thought he'd said it.

'Thanks,' she replied, turning around to face him. 'And good luck.' Only she didn't move away.

He could hear Mrs White in the distance shout out with utter joy, as she caught sight of someone she'd not seen in years.

'I think we should be going,' he said, but he didn't move either. He was conscious he was being examined, that she was looking at him as though she actually approved of what she saw.

'I'm not used to seeing you all dressed up in a suit. I'd forgotten how dark and mysterious you can look.'

'Must be my Mediterranean heritage.'

She smiled. 'Only your bow tie isn't quite straight. Here, let me…'

And before he could protest and tell her he could do it himself, that she was causing a reaction he could do without, on today of all days, she was raising her perfectly manicured nails and giving the material a gentle tug.

'Perfect,' she said with a smile he knew he'd never forget. 'Shall we go and join the others?'

The afternoon vanished into the evening before Isy had time to breathe, let alone stop. Everything had to be spot on and everything was until five past eight, when she received a nudge from one of the hired staff.

The hospital was on the phone. Could they speak to Jack? She glanced across at where he was talking to some blonde. He seemed to be smiling. He seemed to be happy, and she couldn't do it to him. Not yet.

No, she said to the nurse at the other end, he wasn't there, but she was. So, she took the message for him and she waited. She waited until the party was over at nine. Until the last guests had staggered through the door, dragged out by a very apologetic Mrs White.

'Gawd 'elp us, love,' she said to Isy, 'you did us proud. You and that young man of yours.'

He's not mine, Isy was about to say, but what was the point? So, she smiled sweetly and accepted the compliment. Now though she needed to find Jack. She had to close her eyes to the chaos of the festivities, of glasses and food everywhere, and concentrate on the only thing which really mattered. The only person who, if her sources were correct, was hopefully in the dining room.

'Found you!'

He looked up from where he was sitting at one of the tables, talking to Jess and Harry. 'I wasn't aware I was lost?'

She tried to smile. 'Could I have a moment alone please?'

Jess stood up to leave, but Jack put out his arm and drew her back down. 'You guys stay here. We'll go outside.'

Once they were in the hallway, he stopped and Isy could sense she had his full attention. 'So,' he asked, 'what is it you want to say to me?'

She glanced up at him, but she couldn't tell what he was thinking, whether he could read her mind or not. All she knew was that now the time had come, she didn't know how to tell him. So, taking his hands in hers, she pulled him towards her, and kissed him. She kissed him gently at first, and then more provocatively, until she felt him respond, as she knew he would. And she prayed he'd remember this moment, this sweet, tender moment of love, and not the darkness which was to follow.

'Isy,' he began, as soon as she let him go, 'what the…'

'It's your mother. She's worse. Not doing so well. We need to go to London. Now. Tonight.'

And she knew he was drowning. That he was trying to grab hold of the information and to piece it together in a way which would keep him afloat.

'When?'

'An hour ago. I've packed a bag for you. Contacted the B&B. We've got to go.'

'And what about all of this?'

'I'll stay,' came a voice from behind. It was Jess's. 'Harry and I will take charge.'

'Fuck it, Isy. Bloody hell. Fuck it.'

'I know,' she said quietly. 'And, who knows, maybe we will. Later.'

He gave her a glance which told her he would hold her to that. That whatever happened next, this was one memory he was not going to let her wriggle out of. But now, as he tore up the stairs two at a time, he needed to get changed.

Travelling to London on the back of a bike in the middle of winter had never been Isy's idea of fun. She'd suggested taking the Mini. Then she could have brought some of her luggage with her, rather than the backpack she was wearing, but he'd refused. And for once she didn't protest.

She didn't argue when he broke the speed limits either. When she feared she'd die long before his mother, as he tore through the night on a journey she knew they'd never forget.

'You don't have to come in,' he said, once they'd finally reached the hospital.

'No, I know I don't, but I am.'

Clutching her helmet, she followed Jack down the deserted corridors and towards Intensive Care. It was almost three in the morning and she was getting fed up with visiting hospitals in the dead of night, feeling like a vampire on the prowl, awake while everyone else slept. 'I hate hospitals.'

'Everyone hates hospitals, Isy.'

'No, I really do,' she said breaking the silence into which they'd lapsed, while waiting to see the on-call doctor. 'My own mother died in one. I was three and I was taken to see her, to say goodbye. Only she didn't look like my mother and I wouldn't go in, and when I did, I cried.'

She wasn't entirely sure why she was telling Jack this now, after all these years. Why she'd chosen to expose the only secret she'd ever possessed, the guilt of a parting which was far from perfect. But, if it eased the pain, and made him see just how important this moment was, then it was well worth it.

'So that's what this has all been about – all along?'

'No. Yes. Possibly. Maybe. I don't know.' And she didn't. All she knew was that she just wanted to make it right. To make sure he didn't make the same mistakes she'd made.

He held out his hand to her, and she took it. He didn't speak, but he gave it the squeeze she needed, to tell her he understood. And together they went in to see the doctor. Then, a little later, in the high-tech arena of Intensive Care, Isy was introduced to his mother.

'You should sit with her,' she whispered, as the machines churned out the essence of life to those around them.

'And you should go.'

'I can stay, if you want me to?'

He shook his head. 'I can do this better if I know you're not watching.'

With a gentle kiss on his lips, she found herself agreeing. 'I'll be at the flat. I'll keep my phone on, so keep in touch. Promise me you'll keep in touch?'

*

It was the only thing that kept Isy sane, the fact he'd promised. Her phone clasped in her hand as she travelled to Tom's in the back of a taxi. Her mind going over and over what the doctor had said, that his mother had some sort of inflammatory response. Her organs were failing and there was nothing they could do.

'Nothing at all?' Jack had asked, as though he needed the doctor to repeat his diagnosis.

'One per cent chance of survival, I'm afraid.' Which she realised long before he did, was their way of saying there was no chance at all.

She bit back tears, her body shivering with exhaustion as she dragged herself out of the taxi and towards the flat. She knew she should have phoned Tom and warned him she was coming up early. Only tomorrow was now today, and it had all happened so quickly.

Opening the front door, she stepped inside. The hallway was bathed in silence and shadows. She could just make out Tom's coat hanging on the rack. His shoes on the floor, immaculate black loafers next to a pair of high heels. Only the heels weren't hers. Neither was the coat next to Tom's. She'd never have worn anything so furry or heels so high.

And she might have laughed, if only she had the energy. She might have congratulated herself on being right, if only it didn't feel more like a failure than a success. And she knew she had to do something, say something, go somewhere, but it was after four in the morning, and all she really wanted to do was sleep.

'Bella, is that you?' She'd not heard the bedroom door open.

'You do know what time it is, don't you?' Tom said, stepping into the hallway and closing the door behind him.

She tried to brave his indignation with some of her own, but she didn't have the strength. All she could do was look at the shoes, at the coat, and then at him.

'You weren't here, Bella. I was lonely.'

Don't you dare make it about me, she wanted to yell at him, but she couldn't, because it *was* partly about her. Even in her befuddled state, she could still see that. That she was the one who'd moved away, who'd left him to go to Devon. She'd expected him to understand what she was trying to do and wait.

As she looked up at him, in the half-light, she knew she'd asked too much.

'It's all right,' she said quietly, 'I'm not going to make a scene.'

'You can stay here, Bella, of course you can. Tonight.'

But she didn't want to. She knew exactly where she wanted to be. Where she'd always wanted to be. Now all she had to do was go back and tell him.

Chapter 23

'Would you like a cup of something?' Jack was conscious of a voice behind him and for a moment he thought it was his imagination. That he'd transposed the noise of the monitors into something resembling music, a touch of humanity in a machine-driven world.

'No,' he said, 'Thanks. I'm fine.' He glanced across at his mother, at the tracheotomy tube, the drips in her arms, the infusions pumping fluid through her veins, and he knew she'd have hated it, every single minute of it.

No bleeding alcohol, Jackie. What's the point of water without wine?

A glimmer of a smile crossed his lips. A touch of light from God knows where. And he remembered what she'd said to him in the ambulance, when they'd found themselves alone. A battle of words from behind the mask.

'You've gotta promise me something, Jackie. Do you hear? You've gotta get them to pull the bleeding plug this time. I've had enough.'

'You always say this,' he reminded her as well as himself.

'No. This time I bleeding mean it. The pain, it's all the bleeding time and I can't take it no more, do you hear? Do you understand? I can't take it.'

And he could hear the note of desperation in her voice, the finality of what she was asking. Yet, still he hesitated. Still, he wasn't sure.

'You went and did it once,' she gasped, grabbing him by the wrist. 'When you wasn't trying. Only it didn't bleeding work, did it? This time, do something useful and get it bleeding right.'

'Are you sure?' the nurse asked, bringing him back to the present.

Am I sure? How could he ever be sure? 'Is she suffering – is she in pain?'

'She's heavily sedated. She's as comfortable as she can be.'

'But is that enough,' Jack wondered. 'And the antibiotics,' he asked. 'There's no point in trying another course?'

The nurse shook her head. 'We've done everything we can do. I'm so sorry. Her pH is too low. She has lactic acidosis.'

He knew he should ask again what the hell that was, that knowledge was power, but it wasn't here. It was meaningless, because the outcome was still the same.

'Thank you,' he said quietly, as he leant over from where he was sitting and picked up his mother's cold and almost lifeless hand in his. 'Only if there is something you could give her, some more morphine or something, to help her through this, I know she'd thank you.'

And he hoped his mother could hear him. That she'd know he'd done what she'd asked, as the nurse finally understood what he meant. That soon, very soon, it would all be over, and she'd finally be at peace.

Chapter 24

The world was a very different place for Isy that Sunday morning. Christmas was less than two weeks away and she hadn't bought a single present yet. Although why she was worrying about that on today of all days, was beyond her.

She was technically homeless. Single and alone, and desperately, desperately tired. Yet none of that mattered when she thought of Jack, and what he must be going through, all by himself at the hospital.

Racing through the entrance of St Cuthbert's, still clutching her bike helmet in one hand and her backpack and mobile in the other, she found herself, once again, negotiating corridors and lifts, trying to find her destination. Only this time, she actually arrived at where she was meant to be, which was a miracle in itself.

Catching her breath outside the entrance to Intensive Care, she glanced down at her phone. No message, which meant that he was still there. That he *had* to be there, on the other side of the doors, waiting for her, but something held her back.

'I can do this better by myself,' he'd said, 'without you.' And she knew she should be feeling aggrieved, insulted, or any other emotion resembling rejection, but she wasn't. It was as though she finally understood what he meant. What he'd been trying to tell her ever since they'd met. That there were some things in life she couldn't share, no matter how much she wanted to, as she'd never know how it felt to be him.

So, she made herself stay where she was and look for a chair and somewhere to sit. And she was doing just fine, trying to curb her natural curiosity, when a nurse appeared through the doors.

'I remember you,' the woman said, as she stood up to ask her about Jack's mother. 'I'm sorry to tell you that she died an hour ago.'

'An hour ago – are you sure?'

The nurse looked a little taken aback. 'Mrs Mancini? Yes, I'm quite sure. I'm sorry. It was very quick, at the end.'

'And her son, the guy who was with her – is he still here?'

'He left. We gave him the information he needed, about registering the death, and he left.'

'Left?' Isy felt her knees almost buckle from under her. 'And,' she asked, trying to process what the nurse was telling her, 'did… did he say anything? Did he leave a message for anyone?'

The woman shook her head. 'No, I'm afraid he didn't. Why – were you related? Were you close?'

Biting back the tears, she wanted to say she'd thought she was. That, once, they'd been inseparable, but then she realised the nurse was talking about his mother. And so, she shook her head and said no. No, they weren't very close at all.

*

234

Jack couldn't believe the timing of it. That on today of all days his battery had died. His charger wasn't in his bag, and he didn't have a clue what Isy's number was. He couldn't remember Jess's either, and there was no way he was going to phone Frank at five in the morning. So, he did the only thing he could think of doing. He used the payphone to leave a message on the only other number he could remember and hoped Jess would get it. That she'd diverted all office calls to her mobile and she'd contact Isy.

Now all he had to do was go back to the B&B and wait, instead of staring up at Tom's flat, tormenting himself with images he didn't need to see, that he could do nothing to prevent, until she got in touch. He had to put his faith in fate, and hope that for once it went in his favour. That she'd know he'd kept his word. And he was waiting for her to do the same.

Isy was beginning to wonder if there was some divine conspiracy to stop her from sleeping, let alone finding the man she loved.

'If you look at the booking,' she was saying as patiently as she could to someone who was taking her job far too seriously for her liking. 'You'll see that the card used was in my name.'

'But the booking isn't,' the girl was saying. 'I can't give you access to a room that isn't in your name.'

'Can't you at least tell me if Jack is here?'

She shook her head. 'I'm afraid that's confidential information.'

'Even though I booked and paid for it?'

The youngster gave an apologetic shrug and Isy wanted to hit her over the head with the glossy magazine she was reading. Didn't she know what she'd been through? That she'd been to hell and back and that it just kept getting worse? That if Jack wasn't here, she really didn't know where else to look?

'OK,' she said wearily, 'do you have another room I can have? Assuming he's not here – so I can wait for him?'

The girl shook her head with a delicious smile of self-satisfaction, as though she knew the cards were all stacked in her favour, and not Isy's. And Isy was just about to disillusion her with a few tricks of her own, when her mobile went. It was Jess.

'Hi, Isy? Now, keep calm…'

Calm? Isy wanted to shout. *I'm so past calm,* but she didn't. She listened to what Jess had to tell her and when she'd finished, she turned around to the receptionist and looked her squarely in the eyes.

'I know he's up there. Now are you going to wake up the father of my children to be, or do I have to post an online review? And I promise you, if I do, it won't be pretty!'

Jack wasn't sure where he was when the phone sounded. It was a ringtone he didn't recognise, and it took him a few seconds to acclimatise, let alone find the damned thing.

'Yes?' he said sleepily, when he had.

'I've got your…your wife down here.'

'I don't have one.' And then the penny finally dropped. 'Is she clutching a bike helmet?'

'Yes,' came the nervous reply.

And he wanted to laugh. He wanted to open up his lungs and roar with laughter and relief.

'Send her up,' he said. 'For Christ's sake, send her up.'

*

'If you knew, if you had any idea…' Isy started as soon as he'd closed the door behind her, 'of how wo…'

But she didn't get a chance to finish the word, let alone the sentence, because Jack was kissing her. The passion infusing through her with such breathtaking exhilaration that it was all she could do to stay upright let alone remain lucid.

Jack, she began. The name whirling about in her mind like a butterfly on speed, and she knew she ought to voice it, to give it some sort of recognition, but it was impossible. Her mouth was wondrously engaged on a mission of its own, and she had no wish to interrupt it, or cancel the provocation, so she gave up trying.

All her promises of playing it cool, and offering him her condolences were dropped along with her belongings, as she threw herself up at him, as though he were life itself. Every nerve, every cell in her body rising up to meet his; his hands touching her, embracing her, as he prised off her jacket, her jumpers, her slip and her bra.

Her heart racing, in glorious anticipation, as his fingers slipped perilously close to her panties, with the promise of so much more. The hunger, the need to respond surging through her, as she stripped his shirt from out of his jeans, the buckle from his belt, the zip from his flies, revelling in the effect she was having on him, on the sheer magnificence of the man before her.

'I'm so sorry,' she gasped, as he broke off finally to look at her, to really look at her. 'So, so…'

'Not now, Isy, for Christ's sake, not now,' he begged, imploring her not to go there, to tell him what he didn't want to hear. 'Not tonight. It's enough you're here, that you're with me. You *are* with me, aren't you?'

'Of course I am,' she promised, as she pulled him back towards her. 'I've always been with you.' And she willed him to believe her and dismiss that flicker of self-doubt she could see in those eyes. As though any minute he'd wake up and she'd be gone.

'Even when you were with Tom?'

'My heart was always yours.'

And he smiled, a gesture of such tenderness that she wondered how she could ever have thought she'd be happy with anyone else. And she knew, as he wrapped his arms around her, that no one would ever come between them again. Not now. Not ever. Never, as he finally got the chance to show her exactly what she'd been missing.

Epilogue

Everything was perfect, just as it should be. The guests were arriving, champagne was being served. The sun was pushing its way through the gaps of the marquee, saved only by the arrival of a gentle sea breeze.

'I told you we could do it,' Isy was saying as she led her father to his seat. 'That we could host an event for 100 in the garden.'

'I'm not disagreeing, my dear,' he replied, raising his voice against the animated chatter all around him. 'Just promise me that I won't ever have to do this again?'

'You won't, not now you've sold the house in London. You and Auntie can enjoy all the solitude you want when she moves down next month for good. No more parties. No more celebrations, not unless you want them.'

Jack watched as she gave her father a kiss on the cheek, before turning her attention back to him. Those large green eyes were full of such warmth and excitement, that it was all he could do not to take her in his arms, there and then, in front of the whole assembly, and show her just how wonderful she was.

The woman who'd made today possible. Fussing and fretting over everything, just in case she'd missed something, some vital ingredient, that would cause the whole event to collapse like a deck of cards, into the blackest hole of her imagination.

And he loved her for it. He loved everything about her. The energy, the enthusiasm, the attention to detail; the matching of the colours, the blues with the pinks, the flowers with his plants, the whole magical ambiance of a summer's wedding. Their wedding. A day he thought they'd never have.

And he knew he ought to tell her, to try to express what he was feeling, but he choked up every time he opened his mouth. So, he gave up trying, and sat down beside her, a vision of pure sensuality, dressed in a lace and satin concoction of her own design.

'Nervous?' she asked, as he offered her a glass of wine.

'Should I be?'

'There's no escape now.' And to prove it, she gave his thigh a gentle squeeze.

'And if I said I was – nervous that is?'

'Then I would have to do something about it.' She smiled, and before he could resist and remove those fingers, she'd trailed them a little further along his trousers, to where they really shouldn't be.

'Isy,' he managed to get out. 'Behave yourself. I have a speech to make.'

'And later?'

'Later I have something to show you.'

'I know you do,' she conceded with a mischievous twinkle in her eyes.

'Not that,' he tried to explain, moving her hand carefully away from temptation. 'Something else, my darling. Something which I think just might interest you.'

*

Isy was intrigued. 'I thought we'd said no presents?' she began, once the speeches were over, but Jack wasn't listening. He was busy standing up and offering her his hand, the smile on his lips telling her this was one argument she wasn't going to win.

'Don't you think they'll miss us?' she asked, as he led her out of the marquee and back up towards the Hall.

'Yes.'

'And?'

'They'll guess where we are,' he said, as the lanterns lit their way.

'And is that good?'

He spun round to face her, his dark eyes aglow with something she couldn't quite make out. 'Nervous?'

'Who – me?' she retaliated. And then she caught the joke, the reversal of roles. 'Never,' she exclaimed. And to prove it, she kicked off her shoes, and threw him a dare, as she'd done so many times before. Only this time, she didn't wait for him to respond. She picked up her dress, the bundles and bundles of material, and raced past him, the breeze in her hair, the strands so carefully structured, so precisely pinned, falling down, one by one.

'Isy...'

She could hear the note of concern, but she didn't care. There were no rabbit holes now, no freshly dug trench. She didn't stop until she reached the hallway of her home.

'There,' she gasped, lowering her gown with the dignity of a duchess, as Jack grabbed her from behind.

'You're impossible,' he declared, swinging her round to face him, his hands against her waist, his breathing broken, as though he didn't know whether to chastise her or make love to her.

'So,' she asked, staring straight up at him, 'where's my surprise?'

'In here.' He led her towards a desk in the study, where, on top of a pile of files, was a box. The very same box she'd seen under his bed all those months ago. Only this time, there was no padlock.

'It's yours,' he said quietly.

She glanced up at the guarded expression in his eyes, and suddenly she didn't know what to do. Out of all the decisions she'd had to make during the last few months, of whether to move back home, to give up her job and help Jess and Jack with theirs, this was the most difficult.

He was offering her his soul. A peep at his past, at the privacy he'd tried so hard to hide. And she knew she didn't have a choice. She had to open it, this most precious of gifts, on this, the most precious of days.

So, trying not to tremble, she prised open the lid and looked inside.

A dog-eared copy of a child's picture book stared up at her. A bar of out-of-date chocolate. And a small, stained box containing, she guessed, a ring.

'Jack...' she began but she couldn't speak. She couldn't find the words to thank him.

'Disappointed?' he asked.

'Disappointed?' she repeated. And to show him just how wrong he was, she took the items out, one by one, and invited him to talk about them. To tell her about their significance, and what they meant to him.

Then, when he'd finished and she'd put the last object back in the box, she glanced up and saw her father standing in the doorway.

242

'Are you ready, my dears,' he said softly, 'to rejoin the wedding party? Are you ready for the rest of your lives?'

Jack stretched his hand out to hers. 'I am, if you are?'

She smiled up at him. 'Always,' she promised, slipping her hand in his. And, together, they followed her father out of the study, leaving the box and all its memories behind them.

Also by Elly Redding

From award-winning author Elly Redding comes a
fresh, effervescent, passionate romance that reunites Kate,
a London career girl, with Saul, her seriously successful and
gorgeous ex-fiancé…

Praise for *True Colours*

'A truly heart-warming book, that I would
recommend to any lovers of romance.'

Joy Wood – author

'Good storyline. Great, relatable characters. Interesting plot.
Cannot wait to see more from this author.'

Jemma H. – NetGalley reviewer

'Strong characters hooked me in from the start.'

Linda M. – Amazon reviewer

Lightning Source UK Ltd.
Milton Keynes UK
UKHW011457190220
358983UK00002B/71